A Girl named Sherlo

Alice Sherlock, a 12-year-old girl, lived alongside her mother and father in a coastal town in 1941, England. Alice also has an older brother named Tyler, who's been away fighting in World War 2, and the family has just been informed that he is coming home on leave. But then shock hits the town when Tyler is taken into hospital after being stabbed in a vicious attack. The police say it was a failed robbery, but Alice suspects more, given that she's gained a sharp and inquisitive mind from reading her favourite novel, Sherlock Holmes. Alice is determined to use everything she's learned from her literary hero and find out who would hurt her brother. However, the more she looks into what happened during his service, the more she risks finding out a shocking secret that Tyler is hiding.

Written and owned wholly by Matthew James Colfer

Terms and Conditions

LEGAL NOTICE

© Copyright 2023 ©**matthewcolfer**

All rights reserved. The content contained within this book may not be reproduced, duplicated, or transmitted without direct written permission from the author or the publisher. Email requests to kevin@babystepspublishing.com

Under no circumstances will any blame or legal responsibility be held against the publisher, or author, for any damages, reparation, or monetary loss due to the information contained within this book, either directly or indirectly.

Legal Notice:

This book is copyright protected. It is only for personal use. You cannot amend, distribute, sell, use, quote, or paraphrase any part, or the content within this book, without the consent of the author or publisher.

Disclaimer Notice:

Please note the information contained within this document is for educational and entertainment purposes only. All effort has been executed to present accurate, up-to-date, reliable, complete information. No warranties of any kind are declared or implied. Readers acknowledge the author is not engaging in the rendering of legal, financial, medical, or professional advice. The content within this book has been derived from various sources. Please consult a licensed professional before attempting any techniques outlined in this book.

By reading this document, the reader agrees under no circumstances is the author responsible for any losses, direct or indirect, that are incurred as a result of the use of the information contained within this document, including, but not limited to, errors, omissions, or inaccuracies.

Published by Babysteps Publishing Limited All enquires to kevin@babystepspublishing.com

ISBN- 9798327447912

Table of Contents

Chapter 1	1
WW2	1
Chapter 2	11
I'm Coming Home	11
Chapter 3	21
The Case of the Missing Dog	21
Chapter 4	33
A Warm Welcome	33
Chapter 5	49
A Bold Accusation	49
Chapter 6	65
A Stab in the Dark	65
Chapter 7	77
A Guiding Hand	77
Chapter 8	87
The Investigation Begins	87
Chapter 9	99
Police Evidence	99
Chapter 10	115
Time for School	115
Chapter 11	127
The Case of the Stolen Cash Box	127

Chapter 12	147
A Crushing Secret	147
Chapter 13	165
Gathering Proof	165
Chapter 14	177
Deadly Accusations, Deadly Consequences	177
Chapter 15	189
Sharpshooter	189
Chapter 16	205
Focus the Mind	205
Chapter 17	217
To Catch A Spy	217
Chapter 18	231
The Truth is Revealed	231
Chapter 19	245
Wedded Bliss	245

Chapter 1

WW2

The year is 1941, two years after Adolph Hitler invaded Poland and World War 2 was declared on Germany by Great Britain and France. Countries across the globe have been fielding mass lines of young men signing up as Army recruits and being sent to the front lines. Most were from families who fought in the last war, but many others were over-eager and desperate to gain pride and glory from killing Nazis. After reaching the battlefield, they soon regretted how hasty they were. The might of the German Army was relentless; they'd occupied France, Norway, Belgium, Denmark and many other countries. Those in the army who survived the battles were either executed or put into POW camps (Prisoners of War). The civilian populations were allowed to go about their daily lives but under the watchful eyes of the Nazis, who they had to cater to or suffer the deadly consequences.

The Germans had just recently taken the country of Yugoslavia. A small team of British soldiers have been smuggled past the German lines in order to rescue the survivors of a reconnaissance team that was ambushed and captured by the enemy. The team leader is Tyler Sherlock, a young man in his early twenties, and he's assured his men that they will rescue their brothers from the dreaded Nazis because no one gets left behind.

Deep in the wilderness of Yugoslavia, a small area stood a two-story house, which served as an outpost for the detachment of German forces. They'd fortified themselves well with at least three machine guns, several armed patrols inside and outside the house, and one armoured car that made regular trips into the wilderness and came back, usually with supplies or, in this case, captured British soldiers.

As the armoured car returned, it pulled up at the front entrance to the house and was met by a German Officer and several guards. Three British soldiers were thrown from the car, all after taking a beating, cuts and bruises to their faces and bodies. The Officer looked at them and gave a little smirk.

"Welcome, I do hope the ride wasn't too rough," said the Officer.

No one responded.

"You won't talk? Fine with me, we have ways of making you speak. And by the end, you'll be begging us to end your miserable lives," said the Officer.

One of the British soldiers looked up at the Officer; he'd taken the worst of the beatings. He then muttered something.

"Go to hell, Nazi scum!" said the soldier.

The Officer just smirked again and nodded for the guards to take the soldiers inside. They were picked up and dragged into the house, struggling to hold onto the hope that they'd survive. But maybe their bad luck was about to change.

On the edges of the house area, Tyler Sherlock and his squad, a series of men in their early to middle twenties, remained in cover. They'd been taking their time to scout the area and determine the strength of the enemy before making their move. One of the squad, a young private named Andy Walker, came back to them while keeping his head low.

"Did you see them?" asked Tyler.

"They've just arrived; they chucked at least three of them out of the car, then took them inside," said Andy.

"The squad was at least eight men," said Billy as the realisation hit them.

"Alright, everyone, chins up. The mission remains; we rescue our brothers and shut this place down," said Tyler.

"It's going to be a tough one though. They have at least three machine guns on three sides of the house, all on the upper floors. If they spot us, they'll cut us to shreds," said Coltan.

"There's also at least twenty-three of them patrolling the outside; who knows how many more are in the house," said Trevor.

"And that armoured car could cause us a world of pain if its mounted gun starts spraying," said Patrick.

"Alright, guys, I know the situation seems desperate. But we came here to save our boys, and that's what we're going to do. So, here's the plan," said Tyler as the squad huddled together and discussed the next move.

Roughly twenty minutes later, the squad figured out what they would do and got themselves into their positions. The plan would be put into action once the armoured car had driven away and was out of sight; Patrick had gone further down the road and was ready to signal once the car was far enough away to not cause any trouble. Finally, the car revved its engine and set off down the dirt road; the squad readied themselves for the signal.

As the car drove past Patrick and into the distance, he flashed his torch in Tyler's direction, a risky thing to do, but it worked. Tyler aimed his rifle at the machine gunner on his side and fired. He shot the gunner, and Andy and Coltan did the same on their sides. The Nazis began shouting at each other as the squad unleashed a hail of gunfire from all directions. The Nazis fired back but had no direct target to shoot at; they started dropping like flies.

A few shots missed the squad by inches, but they didn't let it stop them; they kept at it until the remaining Nazis retreated inside the house. The squad broke their covers and rendezvoused at the front entrance.

"Nice job, guys; now it's just inside to deal with," said Tyler.

"Remember what we were taught. Go room to room, check your corners and keep an eye out for our boys. And watch each other's backs; we're almost through this," said Tyler.

"Once this is over, the first round's on you?" asked Billy as Tyler smiled.

"Only if you get the second one," said Tyler.

"Okay, guys, good luck," said Tyler as the squad readied themselves.

Tyler, Billy and Coltan breached the front door, while Trevor, Patrick and Andy breached the back. They were quickly met by Nazis spraying bullets at them. But the squad kept going; they made short work of the Nazi guards while having even more near misses. After meeting in the corridor, Trevor's side was directed to the basement to search for the captured soldiers while Tyler's side checked upstairs. More fighting erupted as the Nazi's numbers were dwindling and making every effort for a last stand.

Trevor's side broke through the line in the basement and headed for a large door at the room's far end. Trevor readied himself to open the door as Andy and Patrick took cover at the sides.

Trevor reached for the door handle and (BANG) (BANG). Three to four pistol shots came through the wood; at least two hit Trevor as he fell to the floor.

"Trevor!" shouted Andy as Patrick pulled him to the side.

Andy opened the door and charged in; he found it was some sort of torture room. A Nazi wearing a vest was holding a pistol at one of the soldiers, using him as a human shield. The other two were chained to the wall.

"Don't come any closer, British, or else this nice young man will get his brains splattered all over the walls. You can do one of two things: surrender yourself and become my new subject, or be the reason why this fine young specimen gets to go home to his family in a box. Not that they'll be able to identify him- (BANG)" Andy fired and shot the Nazi in the head.

"You talk too much," said Andy.

Patrick came into the room with Trevor; his body armour had deflected the shots, and he was okay. The three of them started to help the captured soldiers, unchaining and picking them up.

"Sorry we took so long," said Andy.

"Just glad you guys made it," said the soldier, feeling breathless and dehydrated.

Tyler's side managed to secure the upper floor and only had one last room to check. The three of them readied themselves and breached it. It was a sort of map room with three remaining Nazis and the Officer from earlier.

"Don't move, everyone, drop your weapons!" said Tyler as one Nazi tried to defy the order and went to shoot, but Billy was quicker on the trigger.

"Unless the rest of you want to be corpses, drop your weapons now!" said Billy.

The Nazi Officer smirked again and spoke to his men in German; there seemed to be some confusion before he barked an order at them. They all dropped their weapons.

"Very well played, British, we surrender," said the Officer.

Tyler and Billy looked at each other, but they weren't sure how easy that was.

A few minutes later, the Officer and his men had been tied up and placed on their knees in the room. The squad had regrouped and felt good about their success.

"Nice work, everyone; we did really well today," said Tyler.

"Now comes the next question: how do we get our boys out of here?" asked Patrick.

"We'll have to salvage a couple of the vehicles in the yard and quickly before that armoured car comes back," said Billy.

"We can handle that," said Trevor as he winced a bit.

The shots didn't do any damage, but the pain was still there.

"Trevor, you look like you're about to collapse. Take some of the squad with you," said Tyler.

"Can I stay and watch the prisoners?" asked Andy.

"Andy, I don't know if you're ready for this sort of thing. Besides, we need to interrogate this guy before we hand him over to Command," said Tyler.

"I can do it. I've been learning fluent German in case we needed to bluff our way out of trouble; it'll work for interrogating, too," said Andy.

Tyler still wasn't sure.

"I don't mind if Andy wants to take my place. I'll help Trevor and Patrick load up our boys, and then we'll handle the prisoners," said Coltan.

"Very well then, switch with Coltan, Andy," said Tyler as Andy smiled.

"Thank you," said Andy as he took Coltan's place.

Coltan left the room with Patrick and Trevor. Tyler and Billy remained.

"You think this small victory means anything, British? This is a mere hit-and-run attack, useless, wasted. How can you possibly think this is going to help you win the war?" said the Officer.

"We're more capable than you think, Nazi scum!" said Andy as the Officer smirked again.

"I don't like how he keeps smirking at us; it's creepy," said Billy.

"Yeah, they're all a bit creepy," said Tyler.

"Tyler, I think we need to talk," said Billy.

"What about?" asked Tyler.

"You know what about the pact? I'm not comfortable with it," said Billy.

"Billy, this really isn't the time to talk about it," said Tyler.

"Well, when will it be good? You and I are coming up for leave soon, and I'm supposed to just go back and lie to everyone I know?" asked Billy.

"It's not lying, Billy; it's keeping them out of trouble until it's all sorted. Then it'll be worth it in the end," said Tyler.

Andy had turned to look at them and taken his eyes off the Officer, who took this opportunity to reach into his back pocket and pull out a grenade he was hiding. A souvenir from a recent kill.

"But what we did was wrong. I still think the wise thing is to tell Command what happened," said Billy.

"We tell Command not just about what we found but how long we've known about it. They'll just as soon court-martial us than send us home," said Tyler.

"But if we can keep a lid on it until the war is over, then it'll benefit everyone back home; it'll be great," said Tyler.

The Officer pulled the pin out of the grenade while still holding it, but Tyler had pretty good hearing and heard the pin go. He saw the grenade just peeking from behind the officer.

"GRENADE!!" shouted Tyler as he tackled Billy through the door only seconds after the grenade exploded.

Chapter 2

I'm Coming Home

<u>Millstone on Sea, England, 9:00 pm, three weeks later</u>

The coastal town of Millstone on Sea in jolly old England was a quaint little town that housed many friendly and helpful people, with the occasional rude and coarse ones, but very little of them. Millstone was a prosperous place with the use of the cinema, theatre, pubs, and various shops and is well protected by the newly established Home Guard, men both young and old patrolling the town day and night for Nazi spies and saboteurs.

One of the many families living in Millstone is the Sherlocks; their house is a very nice manor located just outside of town along the coastal cliffs but far from the edge. Jack Sherlock is the Lord of the Manor and a retired businessman, a tall and distinguished man of 60yrs with silvery grey hair. He made his money from a contract he signed with the Ministry of Defence during the last war. He had to retire a few months into the second war to look after his wife and young daughter when his eldest son, Tyler, enlisted. Mavis Sherlock, 55 years old with blonde shoulder-length hair curled at the ends, is Jack's wife and works part-time as a cleaning lady at the cinema. She also does the bulk of the grocery shopping. Jack takes over every so often to give her a break, but she always makes sure he has a list and the ration book.

And now the youngest in the family, Alice Sherlock, 12 years old, is a long, honey-blonded, bright young girl with a sense of adventure and mystery, mostly because she read the books of her literary hero, Sherlock Holmes. She liked the fact that they shared the same name, and after buying and being unable to put down his first book, she was hooked. Alice tries to keep up with her studies in school and often does her book reports on Sherlock Holmes; she's gained something of a sharp and inquisitive mind from her reading.

Alice has tried to keep in touch with Tyler, sending him letters at the end of every week. However, the letters only get through; other times, it's weeks before anything comes back. Now, the Sherlocks were anxiously waiting for news of Tyler's leave; he'd brought it up in a previous letter, but since then, they had heard nothing. This was just a regular night for the Sherlocks. Jack and Mavis were both turning in, and Alice had already been sent to bed, but she was not sleeping.

Alice was happily reading another Sherlock Holmes novel and was so engrossed in the story that she'd completely forgotten about going to sleep.

Mavis came up to Alice's room and knocked before entering. She smiled as Alice did the same.

"Alice, you're supposed to be asleep," said Mavis.

"I'm sorry, mother, I got caught up with Mr Holmes," said Alice.

"How many times have I heard that excuse?" said Mavis with a small laugh.

"I know we allow a small extension when it's the weekend, but you still need your sleep, young lady," said Mavis.

"I know, mother, I'm sorry. Can I please just finish this chapter? Mr Holmes and Watson are about to find out where Irene Adler hid the photographs," said Alice.

Mavis had sat on the edge of the bed and smiled.

"Just that chapter; I'll be coming around again in 20 minutes. And I'll expect you to be asleep," said Mavis.

"I will, Mother, I promise," said Alice as Mavis kissed her forehead and walked out of the room.

Alice went back to her reading.

Twenty minutes later, Mavis quietly entered the room again and found the light was off, and Alice was fast asleep. She may be slightly obsessed with Sherlock Holmes, but she always tries to keep her promises. Mavis left the room and soon went to bed with Jack. The house was now quiet.

The next morning, 8:00 am

Jasper, the family butler, was always up at 6:00 am to do some of the house work before the rest of the family woke up. However, Mavis always got up at 7:00 to help prepare breakfast; he didn't mind the assistance, as the Sherlocks had always been good to him. Jasper had served in a few households over the years, but when he was kicked out of the last one after the Lord died and the wife couldn't or didn't want to pay him, he was found by Jack and Mavis, who hired him on the spot. He's always been grateful and tried his best to make the most of his chance.

Jack got up and freshened up before heading down for the breakfast table, then sat down with the morning paper. Alice came down ten minutes after he did. Jasper and Mavis served up breakfast, which consisted of bowls of porridge, glasses of water or milk and a few slices of toast, which they had to share. Just because they lived in a fancy house with lots of money didn't mean they could break the rules of rationing food. Everyone started tucking in, taking care of the butter ration and talking about what they'd be doing the day.

"So, do you have any plans for this morning, Alice?" asked Mavis.

"Actually, I'm meeting Lucy, and we're going to Mr Heskith's house. We promised him we'd help find his dog," said Alice.

"Oh, that's right, I bumped into Albert yesterday at the shops. He was very distraught because Wilmer was missing; he's such a sweet dog, it's a wonder why he'd run away," said Mavis.

"That's why I and Lucy want to get on it as soon as possible; we might be able to find something before the trail goes cold," said Alice.

"The weather said it's supposed to be warm today," said Jasper.

"No, Jasper, it's something Mr Holmes always says. It means that we need to get on the case quickly before any evidence disappears," said Alice.

"Well, I think it's great that you're using your newfound skills well. I'm often hearing from people about how you and Lucy have helped them," said Mavis.

"I'm sure Mr Holmes would be very proud," said Jack.

"Thanks, Dad, thanks, Mum," said Alice as Jasper re-entered the room after checking the front door for the morning post. He was holding a letter in his hand.

"Any post, Jasper?" asked Jack.

"Just one, sir, and it's addressed to Miss Alice. I don't want to get any hopes up, but the handwriting looks very familiar," said Jasper as he handed the letter to Alice.

Alice looked at it and gasped slightly.

"He's right, this is Tyler's handwriting!" said Alice as she opened the envelope and read the letter.

Everyone was quiet, waiting for Alice to tell them what it said. Alice's face lit up, and she smiled brightly.

"Oh my! Tyler says his leave has been approved, and he's coming home this evening!" said Alice with excitement; everyone at the table felt the same.

"That's fantastic! But he was promised leave three weeks ago. Does he say what happened?" said Jack.

"He just says that there was an incident, and Billy got hurt, so he had to stay with him. But Billy's doing better, and he's apparently coming home too; they'll be sharing a train!" said Alice.

"Well then, this calls for an early trip to the shops. Tyler's going to need some good food when he comes back because god knows what they've been feeding him out there," said Mavis.

"I'll do an extra special cleaning, ma'am; make the house look spick and span for Master Tyler's arrival," said Jasper.

"That'll be great, Jasper, thank you," said Mavis.

"Jack, you need to come with me to the shops," said Mavis.

"Oh, Mavis, I was hoping for a quiet morning," said Jack.

"Well, that was before your son came home. We need to look our best; we don't want him thinking we've fallen apart," said Mavis.

"Now come on, we'll do some food shopping and stop at the butchers to see if Mr Jones has any sausages left. Tyler likes his sausages," said Mavis.

"If Dad doesn't want to go, then I can come instead, Mum", said Alice.

"Don't you worry darling, you and Lucy need to find poor Wilmer. Before the trail goes cold, you said. And it'll give you a good story to tell Tyler, won't it?" said Mavis as she kissed Alice on the forehead.

"Now, let's all finish our breakfast before we go," said Mavis.

"Thanks for trying, darling," said Jack.

"Oh goodness, I nearly forgot. One of us has to tell Veronica she'll be overjoyed that Tyler's coming back," said Mavis.

"Lucy and I can pop into her shop when we're done, Mum," said Alice.

"Thank you, Alice. You see, Jack, she volunteered without a single complaint; you could learn a lot from her," said Mavis as Jack went back to reading his paper.

Alice was feeling really excited, not just for Tyler coming home, but that they finally had a reason to be happy and active at the same time. It'd been a while since something like that had happened.

Alice and her parents finished their breakfast, then Jack and Mavis dressed and went out the door to visit the shops. Alice dressed in her favourite multicoloured jumper, which was knitted by her Mum using odds and ends of wool she could find. When she handed it to Alice, she apologised and said it was the best she could do because of the war. But to her mother's surprise, Alice loved it and has worn it ever since.

Alice then went to the front door to put on her fawn-coloured beret, her shoes, and her gas mask bag. Then she was out and headed into town to meet Lucy.

Millstone on Sea, Morning, 8:30 am

Alice walked down the coastal path from her house, and another path led down to a beach area, which was one of the reasons they bought the property. Alice made it into town and walked the streets of people who were mostly locals, families, and children making the most of the weekend and Home Guards doing daytime patrolling. Alice smiled and waved to a few people she passed by, some she knew socially and others she'd helped in the past.

Alice then came up to one of her favourite places, the local bookshop, and standing outside was another 12yr old girl with bob-length curly brown hair, Lucy Porter, wearing a blue beret and a similar style jumper but consisting of shades of blue in contrast to Alice's much brighter colours.

"Hey, Lucy," said Alice.

"Hey Alice," said Lucy as she came over.

"You're looking a little brighter, Alice," said Lucy.

"I've just had some amazing news. Tyler is coming home today!" said Alice.

"Oh, that's fantastic!" said Lucy as she and Alice hugged.

"We haven't seen Tyler around for nearly…two years?" said Lucy.

"Just about two and a half since he signed up. And aside from the letters we've sent to each other, this is the first time he's been granted leave," said Alice.

"I bet your Mum and Dad were thrilled by the news," said Lucy.

"Of course they were. Mum's even taking Dad to do some quick shopping for tonight's tea. Dad wasn't as pleased as he'd hoped for a quiet morning," said Alice.

"So, do you need to do anything? Can I help?" asked Lucy.

"No, Mum's orders, stick to the case and help Mr Heskith find his dog," said Alice.

"Well then, what are we waiting for?" said Lucy as she and Alice started walking.

"Oh, by the way, we have to stop at the sweet shop to tell Veronica about Tyler," said Alice.

"Sounds good. Make a young woman's day, find a missing dog and buy some sweets as a reward. I love this job," said Lucy playfully.

Alice and Lucy had been best friends since they first met in school. They are both bright and fun-loving people, but one ironic thing is that they have a similar interest in Sherlock Holmes. They loved the books so much that they even started solving their own little mysteries around town, searching for missing pets and misplaced items. But everyone they helped was always very thankful and appreciative of what they did for them.

Still, Alice longs for the day when she can solve a real and complex mystery, just like Mr Holmes.

Chapter 3

The Case of the Missing Dog

Mr Heskith's House, Morning, 8:35 am

Mr Albert Heskith had a one-story bungalow with a small garden area. He liked growing his flower bed for everyone to see, but he wished it could be bigger. The backyard was mostly for his dog, Wilmer, to run around in, and a gate at the side kept him from getting out and into the street. So how Wilmer had gotten past the gate and where he was now is what Alice and Lucy hoped to solve.

The girls approached the front gate as they saw Mr Heskith watering his flowers.

"Morning, Mr Heskith," said Alice as Mr Heskith turned and smiled.

"There they are, the little mystery solvers. Come on in, girls," said Mr Heskith as Alice and Lucy came through the gate.

"I'm really glad you're both here. Wilmer is still missing, and no one has seen him," said Mr Heskith.

"We'll try our best to help, Mr Heskith. But first, we need to know the facts from the beginning," said Alice.

"Yes, of course. Well, I just let Wilmer out into the backyard like I always do every morning and afternoon and let him stretch his legs a bit. They're the only times he gets any exercise," said Mr Heskith.

"Don't you take him for walks?" asked Lucy.

"Unfortunately, not too often anymore. Since my late wife Margaret passed, God rest her soul (Mr Heskith did the Christian sign, and Alice and Lucy did the same), I've had to take the responsibilities of the house. Paying the bills, grocery shopping and watering my flowers," said Mr Heskith.

"And lately, whenever I take Wilmer for a walk, my back starts killing me. Wilmer wants to run all around the park, but my back won't let me keep up with him. He really liked those walks," said Mr Heskith.

"Did you see a doctor about your back?" asked Lucy.

"I did go to see the local doctor, and he told me it was hurting because of age. I said to him, "You cheeky sod, I'm only sixty-six; I'm still active and alive". He wasn't convinced though" said Mr Heskith.

"Anyway, I let Wilmer out into the backyard yesterday morning at about 8:00 am and came back maybe an hour or so later. I looked around the yard and couldn't find him; it was like he'd just vanished," said Mr Heskith.

"You have a side gate, right?" asked Alice.

"I do. I keep it locked when Wilmer is outside, so he doesn't run into the street and hurt himself," said Mr Heskith.

"Can we see it?" asked Alice.

"Sure, follow me", said Mr Heskith as he led Alice and Lucy round the side of his house and showed them a wooden gate with a metal lock.

Alice started to check the gate and how secure the lock was.

"Do you think that Wilmer might have run away, or maybe someone took him?" asked Lucy.

"I wouldn't have thought so; you don't hear about dog-napping around these parts. As for him running away, well...I wouldn't have considered it, but I don't know," said Mr Heskith.

Alice then had a thought.

"Mr Heskith, you said you don't know how Wilmer got past the locked gate, right?" asked Alice.

"That's right" replied Mr Heskith.

"Forgive me for asking this, but is it possible that maybe you..forgot to lock the gate?" said Alice as Mr Heskith thought for a moment.

"Oh no, I think you may be right. I did have a lot on my mind yesterday; I got behind on a bill and was trying to figure out how to resolve it. I must have forgotten to lock it," said Mr Heskith.

"Well, at least we know how Wilmer got out. Now the question is, where did he go afterwards?" said Alice as they all went back to the front of the house.

"Let's think. Wilmer got past the gate; this was familiar territory, but he wouldn't just leave alone. Not unless something compelled him to," said Alice.

"Could he have seen someone he knew? But they wouldn't take him without asking Mr Heskith," said Alice.

"There are no obvious footprints on the lawn, and Wilmer would've sounded the alarm if someone had tried to take him," said Lucy.

Alice was about to say something when she saw Mr Jones's butcher's van drive past, the meat logo on the side showing steak and sausages. A thought struck her.

"Mr Heskith, does that van always drive by?" asked Alice.

"Mostly, yeah, it's his route," said Mr Heskith as Alice ran out the gate and down the street.

"Lucy, we have to follow that meat van!" said Alice as she kept running.

"We'll be back, Mr Heskith. Alice, wait for me!" said Lucy as she ran to catch up with Alice.

"Good luck, girls," said Mr Heskith.

Alice and Lucy chased the meat van down the street until it finally stopped outside a house. Mr Jones, the town butcher, got out and retrieved a delivery from the back of the van. He walked up to the front door and knocked; he handed the bag to a woman who answered, exchanged some pleasantries and started walking back, just in time for Alice and Lucy to catch up, both out of breath.

"Mr Jones," said Alice breathlessly.

"Alice, Lucy, what's going on?" asked Mr Jones.

"We need...to ask you...about Wilmer," said Lucy breathlessly.

"Wilmer, Albert's dog?" asked Mr Jones.

"Yeah, we're trying to find him," said Alice.

"Okay, girls, catch your breath and then explain the situation to me," said Mr Jones as Alice and Lucy took a moment and recovered slightly.

"Mr Heskith's dog is missing, and when I saw your van, I thought that maybe it's possible he saw the meat sign and perhaps ran after you," said Alice.

"Well, it's possible, I suppose, but I don't recall seeing a dog chasing me. Then again, I'm usually keeping my eyes on the road, and I don't look around as much when making the deliveries," said Mr Jones.

"How often do you make deliveries?" asked Alice.

"Every third Friday and Saturday morning, depending on whether I can get the petrol," said Mr Jones.

"Maybe Wilmer was following from a distance; how long does your route last?" asked Lucy.

"I have about five more houses to do. It's a lot of twisting and turning around town, then back to my shop, but it takes me no more than an hour," said Mr Jones.

"Do we have to search five houses for Wilmer?" asked Lucy.

"One of them might have seen him; I think we have to," said Alice, not too keen on the idea herself.

"Well, I'll tell you what. Maybe we can work something out as it's for a good cause. I'll give you girls a lift in my van to each of the houses and back to my shop, but you have to help me with making my deliveries, deal?" said Mr Jones.

Alice and Lucy looked at each other and nodded.

"Deal," said Alice as she and Lucy shook Mr Jones's hand.

The next hour followed with Alice and Lucy riding with Mr Jones to the five houses and helping to carry his deliveries. There wasn't much, but the help was appreciated. They also asked each of the recipients if they'd seen Wilmer, and four of them all said no. But their luck had turned around by the fifth house as Mr Jones made his final delivery.

"Thank you, Mr Jones; my hubby will be happy to have his brisket ration," said Mrs Wilson.

"You're welcome, Mrs Wilson," said Mr Jones.

"Mrs Wilson, we're looking for a dog named Wilmer. He belongs to Mr Heskith, and he's missing. Did you perhaps see a dog chasing Mr Jones's van?" said Alice.

"Funnily enough, I did. Just moments after you drove away, Mr Jones, this dog started running after you. I tried to wave you down, but you didn't see me," said Mrs Wilson.

"Where would you have gone after here?" asked Alice.

"Back to the shop to open up," said Mr Jones.

"Then that's the next port of call," said Lucy as everyone headed for the van.

"Thank you, Mrs Wilson," said Alice.

"You're welcome, dearie; best of luck," said Mrs Wilson as the van drove away shortly afterwards.

Mr Jones Butcher's Shop, Morning, 9:36 am

Alice and Lucy rode with Mr Jones back to his shop, a nice little place with plenty of room for customers and always something on display; sometimes, it's plaster.

Mr Jones opened the front door and entered the shop; Alice and Lucy followed.

"I still don't see how a dog could've gotten inside without me noticing," said Mr Jones.

"It's very easy to do; dogs are clever animals. I heard about one who was sheltered in this family's home all night, and they never discovered him until the next morning," said Lucy.

"Okay, Mr Jones, what is happening now? What do you usually do?" asked Alice.

"Well, I check inside the cold room to see what meat I have for the ration books, then I just do some quick sweeping up and wipe down the windows a bit. Change the sign to open and ready myself and my assistant Raymond for the influx of customers," said Mr Jones.

"He has to be somewhere, maybe-Wait. Did you say you checked inside the cold room?" said Alice.

"Yes, I'm only in there for a couple-Oh no!" said Mr Jones as he realised what Alice was trying to say.

He reached for his keys and opened the cold room door. Everyone went inside and started looking around for Wilmer.

Finally, they all came back out, shivering a bit, but no sign of Wilmer.

"He's not in there," said Alice.

"Thank goodness, I don't think I can stand the sight of a frozen dog," said Lucy.

"Well, Mr Jones is right; there are not many other places to hide here. Where could that dog be?"

said Alice as the door to the shop opened up, and a young boy, 11 years old, came in.

"Is everything alright, Mr Jones?" he asked.

"Um, a bit complicated, Raymond. Might be a slight delay opening the shop," said Mr Jones.

"Uh, okay then. Mr Jones, I'm sorry to ask this, but can I have an extra sausage ration today?" said Raymond.

"Why do you need an extra sausage?" asked Mr Jones.

"Well, you see, I found this dog yesterday. I think he'd been trapped in the cold room for an hour, and I wasn't sure how the customers would react, so I smuggled him out the back and took him home," said Raymond as Alice and Lucy looked at each other.

"Is he okay?" asked Lucy.

"I think so. My Mum gave him loads of blankets to warm up, and he ate my sausage ration, so that's why I'm asking for more," said Raymond as Alice and Lucy smiled.

"Raymond, you're a genius," said Mr Jones as Raymond managed a small smile, not that he understood what was going on.

A short while later, Alice and Lucy went with Raymond to his house just across the road from the shop. They were stroking the dog he'd found, looking healthy and well. Mr Jones had phoned Mr Heskith and gone to fetch him.

"I really hope this is Wilmer; he's such a friendly dog," said Lucy.

"I hope so too, but I think there's a good chance," said Alice.

Mr Heskith was led inside by Raymond's mother; his face widened with a big smile.

"Wilmer, there you are, boy," said Mr Heskith as Wilmer suddenly got up and ran into his arms.

"Thank you, both of you girls; you have no idea how much this means to me," said Mr Heskith.

"It was our pleasure, but Raymond is the real hero here. He made sure Wilmer was still around for us to find," said Alice.

"Thank you, Raymond, for looking after my dog," said Mr Heskith.

"You're welcome, sir; it's been great to have a dog around the house, especially one as friendly as Wilmer", said Raymond.

"Mr Heskith, maybe there's a way you can show Raymond just how grateful you are for looking after Wilmer," said Lucy.

"Oh, I think you're right," said Mr Heskith.

"Um, Raymond? As a proper thanks for saving Wilmer and taking good care of him, how would you like to see him a bit more often?" asked Mr Heskith.

"Really?" said Raymond.

"Well, my back means I can't go out as often anymore, and I know Wilmer is missing his walks. So it would be a comfort knowing that there's someone who can take him out for a while and play in the park for a bit, something that'll make all three of us happy," said Mr Heskith.

"Yes, yes sir, I'd love that," said Raymond with a big smile.

"Speaking of which, Raymond, can you hold Wilmer for a moment?" asked Mr Heskith as he handed Wilmer to Raymond.

"I think that you girls deserve a sort of reward for finding Wilmer," said Mr Heskith.

"There's no need, Mr Heskith, we're not in this for rewards," said Alice.

"No, no, I insist. Now, it's not much, but hold out your hands," said Mr Heskith as Alice and Lucy held out their hands.

"Here you are, a half crown for each of you," said Mr Heskith.

"Thank you," said Alice and Lucy.

They left the house a few minutes later and started walking down the street, feeling good about another case solved and a job well done.

"Now, I don't know about you, but are we both thinking of where to spend our half-crowns?" asked Lucy.

"Elementary, my dear Lucy," said Alice as they both laughed.

Chapter 4

A Warm Welcome

<u>Millstone on Sea Sweet Shop, Morning, 10:00 am</u>

Alice and Lucy headed for the Sweet shop; they liked going there but didn't buy sweets as often as all the other kids; unlike the rest, they liked their teeth where they were. This was also the place where Veronica Fox worked; she was Tyler's girlfriend, and they'd been together for a year before the start of World War 2. Since then, just like the rest of the Sherlocks, she'd barely heard from him, except the letters Alice would read to her; they often mentioned the both of them.

Alice and Lucy entered the shop and were greeted by the sweet atmosphere, pun intended. Containers of lemon sherbets, barley sugar twists, liquorice, cola cubes and ration chocolate. And plenty of kids were admiring and buying lots of them.

The owner was Miss Bailey, but a lot of kids called her Miss Sweet, given her friendly and kind nature towards them.

"Hello, Miss Bailey," said Alice.

"Ah, hello, young Alice, and you too, Lucy," said Miss Bailey.

"Hello, Miss Bailey, we'd like to buy some sweets," said Lucy.

"A special occasion, is it?" asked Miss Bailey.

"Another case solved, and a dog reunited with his owner," said Alice.

"Well, if that isn't a reason to celebrate, I don't know what it is. Go on then, see what you'd like," said Miss Bailey as Alice and Lucy started to browse the selections.

"Oh, Miss Bailey, is Veronica in today? There's something really important I need to tell her," said Alice.

"Yes, she's just in the stock room. I'll fetch her for you," said Miss Bailey.

"Thanks," said Alice as she started eyeing up the ration chocolate; she could never resist the milky taste.

Veronica came out of the storeroom shortly afterwards; she was a nice and pretty young lady in her twenties with orange curly hair.

"Hey Alice, Miss Bailey said you need to talk to me," said Veronica.

"We had a letter this morning from Tyler," said Alice.

"Is he okay? Has something happened to him?" asked Veronica, nearly panicking herself.

"No, no, he's fine, the news is good. His leave has been approved; he's coming home this evening," said Alice.

"Oh my gosh!" said Veronica as she and Alice started jumping with excitement.

"Oh, that's wonderful; I haven't seen him in so long. Oh my stars, my hair's a mess, and I haven't done any makeup; what's he going to think when he sees me?" said Veronica.

"Veronica, you're over thinking it. The most important thing is that Tyler is coming home, and he'll be really pleased to see you," said Alice as Veronica smiled.

"But, if you like, we could always get you a makeover," said Lucy.

"That's sweet, Lucy, but it's this evening, and I don't think the salon makes last-minute bookings," said Veronica.

"I meant us; we have experience," said Lucy.

"Yeah, how do you think we stay this pretty?" said Alice as she and Lucy smiled.

Veronica's unsure thoughts quickly disappeared, and a confident smile filled her face instead.

Millstone on Sea Train Station, Evening, 8:00 pm

The train station could be a place for happiness or sadness. Some trains contained young recruits and soldiers departing for the front lines and saying goodbye to their families and loved ones. But other trains contained similar passengers who were coming back, either on leave or because they'd been discharged or gone AWOL. Either way, they were always greeted with joy and excitement. Alice, her parents and Veronica were waiting for Tyler's train to arrive at the platform. Mavis and Jack had done a good amount of shopping for the night's meal, and Alice and Lucy had fun doing Veronica's makeup; she was very impressed with the results. Lucy sadly had to go home afterwards as she was supposed to help her Mum with some house chores, but she promised to come by tomorrow to see Tyler.

The train pulled into the station, and Jack checked his pocket watch.

"Its 8:00, so this should be the right train", said Jack.

"I really hope he didn't miss it," said Mavis.

As a load of people started to disembark from the train, being greeted and gradually led away, Alice kept scanning the crowds, and at the other end of the platform, she saw him.

"There he is, Mum, it's Tyler!" said Alice with excitement.

"You go ahead, sweetheart, we'll catch up," said Mavis as Alice charged off, pushing her way through the crowds to the final carriage where Tyler was stepping off with his kitbag.

"TYLER, TYLER!" shouted Alice.

Tyler spotted her, and his face lit up.

"There's my sister!" said Tyler as Alice ran into his arms. He picked her up and hugged her tightly.

"Oh, Alice, you've grown bigger; stop it," said Tyler.

"I missed you so much, Tyler," said Alice.

"I missed you too, little sister, though not so little anymore", said Tyler as he put Alice down again. It was hard for them to let go of each other.

"You look great," said Tyler.

"So do you," said Alice.

"Liar," said Tyler with a laugh.

He then looked up to see his parents coming through the crowd.

"Hey, my darling," said Mavis as she hugged Tyler tightly.

"Hey, Mum, it's great to see you," said Tyler, and they both stopped hugging after a moment.

"Welcome home, son," said Jack as he and Tyler hugged.

"Thanks, Dad, it's great to be home," said Tyler as they also stopped after a bit.

Tyler looked past everyone and saw Veronica; she seemed a bit unsure how he would react to her. But Tyler smiled and hugged her as well.

"I wasn't sure if you'd come," said Tyler.

"Of course I came," said Veronica as they stopped hugging.

"Veronica, you look as beautiful as ever. In fact, you look dazzling," said Tyler.

"Well, I got some help from Alice and Lucy doing my makeup," said Veronica.

"Nice job, Alice," said Tyler as Alice smiled.

"Veronica, is your lipstick smudged?" asked Tyler.

"It is?" asked Veronica.

"Let me help with that," said Tyler, embracing Veronica and kissing her. She didn't object at all. But Alice did turn away a little.

"Oh, Tyler," said Veronica as he'd stopped, and she giggled a bit.

"Okay, come on now, lovebirds, this young soldier needs to get home," said Jack.

"Oh, speaking of which. Mum, do we still have the spare room at the house?" asked Tyler.

"We do, why?" asked Mavis.

"There's someone I'd like to stay over for a while," said Tyler.

"Who?" asked Jack as Tyler looked behind them.

Everyone turned around to see the person Tyler was talking about; it was Billy with his left arm bandaged in a sling. He was also in his early twenties.

"Billy Desmond," said Mavis.

"Hello, Mrs Sherlock," said Billy as Alice ran over and gave him a hug.

"Thanks for the love, Alice. I'm surprised you remember me," said Billy.

"You're Tyler's best friend; how could I forget you?" said Alice.

"Billy, of course, you're welcome to stay with us," said Mavis.

"Thank you, Mrs Sherlock, I really appreciate it," said Billy.

"And for heaven's sake, call me Mavis; you've earned that," said Mavis.

"Very well, Mavis," said Billy.

"Alright, come on, everyone. We've got a big dinner waiting for all of us, so let's get home before it goes cold," said Jack as everyone started to leave the station, still making small talk as they made the journey back home.

The Sherlock Household, Evening, 8:15 pm

Everyone arrived back at the house and went inside. Jasper greeted everyone.

"It's good to see you home, Master Tyler," said Jasper as he shook hands with Tyler.

"Great to see you, Jasper. I'm glad you haven't left us for greener pastures," said Tyler.

"Oh, this old place would fall apart without me, Master Tyler", said Jasper.

"And Master Billy, too; good to see you as well, sir," said Jasper as he shook hands with Billy.

"Hello, Jasper. This house looks great. Have you been around with the duster again?" said Billy.

"Duster, mop, sponge and vacuum cleaner, just another day in the life of a dedicated butler," said Jasper.

"How's the meal looking, Jasper?" asked Mavis.

"Nearly ready to be served Ma'am. But I could use some help with the serving bit," said Jasper.

"Of course, everyone, go find your place at the table. Dinner will be served shortly," said Mavis.

"Mind if I lend a hand?" asked Tyler.

"You don't have to, Master Tyler. I'm sure that you're tired from your journey," said Jasper.

"Yeah, but you've put all this effort into me, and I'd like to do my bit for the family. Plus, I can smell freshly cooked sausages a mile away, so I'd like to make sure they're done right," said Tyler with a smile.

"Very well, Master Tyler," said Jasper, smiling as he, Mavis, and Tyler entered the kitchen.

Everyone else went into the dining room and found their places. Billy seemed to struggle a bit until Alice helped him to sit down.

"Thank you, Alice," said Billy.

"It's okay. Do you need anything for your arm? I can get the first aid box," said Alice.

"No, it's okay. You're kind, but the doctor told me just a few more days, and I can take it out of the sling. Just make sure I don't lift anything heavy or try to do a handstand, and I'll be fine," said Billy as he and Alice laughed a little.

"How did you hurt your arm?" asked Alice.

"Cut by some shrapnel from a grenade that went off," said Billy.

"Oh, that's horrible," said Alice.

"Well, the doctor said I was lucky to have just been cut. If it hadn't been for Tyler, I could've been in worse condition," said Billy.

"What did Tyler do?" asked Alice.

"We'd just captured these Germans, and this officer among them had a grenade hidden up his sleeve. He pulled the pin, but thanks to Tyler's good hearing, he grabbed me and tackled me through the door only seconds before it went off. He saved my life," said Billy.

"That sounds like my brother," said Alice.

"Dinner is served," said Jasper as he, Mavis and Tyler began delivering the plates of food to the table.

The sausages were mainly for Tyler, but he convinced Jasper to give the other one to Alice. It was a series of vegetables with some Chicken and Ham pie for everyone else. Everyone started tucking in and chatting with each other about events at home, not so much on the war front; it was a subject that soured the atmosphere.

However, Tyler was able to fit in one story about a private who wanted to prank the officer in charge for being rude to him. He found that the officer had his own little step in the camp, where he would always make his stance before addressing the men. No one knew why he liked that step so much, but it gave the private an idea. He got some bird seeds that would be fed to the carrier pigeons delivering orders to the camp and spread them over the step. The next morning, the officer was furious about his step being covered in birds and their droppings; he demanded an explanation, and the private said, "It looks like your step has flown the coop, sir". Everyone at the table had an uproar of laughter, and it was an exciting dinner.

Afterwards, everyone had finished up and retired to the living room. Veronica had to leave because it was late, but she agreed to return tomorrow as the family had planned an outing. Mavis dug out an old photo album and was showing pictures of Tyler growing up, then his friendship with Billy and the arrival of Alice. It was more than enough to get some embarrassed faces around the sofa. By this point, everyone was looking a bit tired.

"Okay, everyone, I think our beds are calling," said Mavis.

"If you'd like to follow me, Master Billy, I'll show you to the guest room," said Jasper.

"Thank you, Jasper, goodnight all," said Billy with a yawn as he left the room.

"Come on, Alice, time for bed, sweetheart," said Mavis.

"No, Mum, I want to stay up with Tyler a bit longer," said Alice.

"Honey, you need your sleep. Especially if you want to be wide awake for tomorrow's outing," said Mavis.

"But Mum...." said Alice.

"Okay, I'll tell you what, Alice. If you go upstairs, brush your teeth and get into bed, how about I read you some Sherlock Holmes as a bedtime story?" said Tyler.

"Okay," said Alice as she raced out of the room.

"Nicely done," said Jack as Tyler smiled and left the room. Jack and Mavis left shortly afterwards.

After a few minutes, Alice was tucked up in bed, ready for Tyler as he entered the room.

"Hey, little sis," said Tyler as he sat on the edge of the bed.

"Hey, big brother," said Alice.

"So, you brushed your teeth?" asked Tyler.

"I did," said Alice.

"Thoroughly?" asked Tyler as Alice showed her teeth.

"Pearly white, well done. Now then, let's see what Mr Holmes is up to," said Tyler as Alice handed him the book from her nightstand.

"Ah, I believe I started this book a while back, but I only got halfway through," said Tyler.

"You don't have to read it if there's going to be spoilers," said Alice.

"It's no worry, Alice; I'm sure I'll remember the plot as I go along," said Tyler, opening the book and going to the page with the bookmark.

"I'm really glad you're home, Tyler," said Alice as Tyler smiled and held her hand.

"Me too, little sis," said Tyler as he started reading.

Before leaving for the war, Tyler used to read a lot to Alice; he had a way of doing almost convincing English accents for both Holmes and Watson. It always brought a smile to Alice's face and kept her interested, and it even worked to put her to sleep as

Tyler looked and saw she was sleeping soundly. He carefully removed his hand from hers, put the book back and snuck out of the room.

As Tyler closed the door, he nearly jumped out of his skin when Billy suddenly appeared next to him.

"Ah, Billy, you scared me," said Tyler.

"We need to talk; Tyler and I are not taking no for an answer," said Billy.

"Shh, Alice is sleeping. Okay, let's talk outside; just keep your voice down," said Tyler as he and Billy headed out of the house.

They walked a little way along the coastal path before stopping.

"Okay, Billy, what's bothering you?" asked Tyler.

"What's bothering….Tyler, how can you just sit there with your family who hug you tightly and give you a nice welcome home dinner and still lie to them about what we know?!" asked Billy.

"Billy, I told you everything is fine. I sent a letter to Coltan's smuggler friend, and he replied before we left for our train," said Tyler.

"And what did he say?" asked Billy.

"That the, you know what is secure in a safe place, and he'll keep an eye on it until we come to collect at the end of the war," said Tyler.

45

"I still don't feel comfortable leaving the, you know what, in the hands of a criminal, regardless of Coltan's trust in him", said Billy.

"He's not a criminal; he's a gentleman smuggler. And Coltan is not the only one who trusts him; many other men in the camps are thankful for the things he's gotten for them," said Tyler.

"Okay, look, I didn't ask you out here to talk about whether smugglers are criminals or not. I want to talk about what happened three weeks ago," said Billy.

"Ah, yes, three weeks ago," said Tyler with some sadness in his voice.

"Tyler...Andy died because of us because we let our guard down. We're supposed to be brothers, watching each other's backs....we failed him," said Billy.

"We didn't fail him, Billy; I failed him; I let my guard down first. I should've realised that a smirking German officer would have a trick up his sleeve; we're supposed to check for that. And I knew that Andy wasn't ready to guard prisoners of that high calibre, but I thought it would give him the experience," said Tyler.

"You know, I wasn't the only one who didn't like what we were doing, Andy agreed with me. And we were going to try to convince you after the mission," said Billy.

"Tyler, what we did was wrong; what we're doing now is still wrong. And with Andy gone, I still think the best thing is to tell the Home Office while we have the chance," said Billy.

"Look, Billy, I hear everything you're saying, and in all honesty, I have had similar doubts. But it's like I said, we're in too deep to back out now," said Tyler.

"If we tell them everything, it'll mean court martial, followed by years of imprisonment or death by firing squad. And I won't put Alice through that, or Veronica, or Mum and Dad," said Tyler.

"I know it sounds like I'm being selfish, but I swear I'm not. I'm doing this for the squad and our families; it'll be great for all of us. And we'll even do something for Andy, give him a proper memorial or a place named after him," said Tyler.

"You believe what I'm saying, right brother?" asked Tyler.

Billy was quiet for a moment before he answered.

"I believe you, and for what it's worth, I respect what you're saying," said Billy.

"Now, forgive me for saying this, but it needs to be said. If either you or anyone else on the squad tries to renege the pact and take them, you know what, for yourselves, I'm telling the Home Office everything and to hell with the consequences," said Billy.

"Okay, Billy, I promise that's not what we're about; we'll stick to the pact. Now come on, let's get some sleep," said Tyler as he led Billy back to the house.

The secret being kept by Tyler, Billy and the rest of the squad turned out to be bigger than first thought. Something that would earn them all a court martial if it was found out. But whatever it was is yet to be discovered.

Chapter 5

A Bold Accusation

The next morning, 10:00 am

The morning broke as the Sherlocks were preparing for their outing, a trip to the beach. Veronica was coming and offered to pass an invitation to Lucy so she could join, too. Mavis and Jasper had put together a picnic basket of sandwiches and one of Mavis's famous jam sponge cakes. Everyone else was getting ready in their beach clothes and packed their swimsuits for a splash in the sea.

Veronica arrived just as everyone was ready to go; Lucy was with her.

"Hey Alice," said Lucy.

"Hey Lucy, are you ready for today?" said Alice.

"Well, I'm not wearing all this for a fancy dress party, so yeah," said Lucy as she noticed Tyler.

"Tyler," said Lucy.

"Hey, Lucy," said Tyler as they hugged each other.

"It's great to see you, Lucy; you look good," said Tyler.

49

"Thanks, so do you," said Lucy.

"Oh, and thanks for looking out for my sister while I've been away," said Tyler.

"That's okay, but at times, it felt like she was looking out for me," said Lucy as she also noticed Billy.

"Billy?" said Lucy.

"Hey, Lucy," said Billy as they hugged.

"Ow! Mind the arm, sorry," said Billy.

"Are you okay? What happened?" asked Lucy.

"Just a little injury, nothing to worry about," said Billy.

"Now come on, everyone, let's get to that beach," said Billy.

"My thoughts exactly; let's go!" said Tyler as everyone was out the door and headed for the beach.

After setting up the picnic area, underneath two parasols, Alice, Lucy, Tyler and Veronica changed into their swimsuits and all charged into the sea, laughing loudly and splashing each other with such fun and excitement, something that they hadn't had for a long time. Billy remained back with Mavis and Jack, helping to set out the sandwiches and slices of cake.

"Are you sure you don't want to join them for a splash?" Jack asked Billy.

"I'd love to, sir, but I can't get this sling wet, doctor's orders," said Billy.

The splashing in the sea lasted for nearly an hour; everyone was just having so much fun. But they did stop once their stomachs started growling. They left the water and went back to the picnic area, and then everyone happily tucked into the sandwiches and the cake, still managing some laughs while trying not to choke on the food. Alice and Lucy even managed some sandcastle building with a little help from Tyler and Veronica.

The rest of the day was followed by a lot more fun. A long walk through Millstone's vast countryside to help the food go down, a stand-up comedy act at the theatre, Charlie Cheeseman and the Cheerful Chums, some lunch and playing in the playground at the park. Even Raymond showed up with Wilmer and had an excitable time with them.

George and Dragon Pub/Inn, Evening, 8:00 pm

Finally, the evening arrived, and the family settled down for a drink at George and Dragon. A rather cosy place with good service, a talented piano player and rooms available to all. The pub's clientele usually consisted of everyday locals, Home Guard members, and soldiers on leave. The landlord was Mr Joe Prosser, and the barman was Tim Perkins. Mr Prosser brought over another round of drinks on the house for war veterans and their families. Normally, 12-year-old girls weren't allowed in pubs, but Tyler was able to convince Mr Prosser to make an exception.

The pub door opened, and in walked a man in his late seventies with grey hair and a beard; he was wearing an old army uniform.

"Hey, look, its Old Boy", said one of the patrons.

"Any Germans out there, old timer? What did you do, chase them away with your walking stick and shout "You rotten Nazis!" at them?" said another patron as they both laughed.

The man said nothing; he just shrugged it off and asked for a half at the bar. Tyler got up and approached him.

"Mr Nesbit?" said Tyler as he turned and his face lit up.

"Tyler Sherlock, who let you back into town?" said Mr Nesbit. He got up and hugged Tyler.

"How are you, my boy?" asked Mr Nesbit.

"I'm good, Mr Nesbit. I see the Old Boy nickname still hasn't faded," said Tyler.

"I'm afraid not. I think it's here to stay, at least as far as these gits are concerned," said Mr Nesbit.

"Oh, we're just laughing, Old Boy, no offence intended", said one of the patrons picking on him earlier.

"So how long are you back for?" asked Mr Nesbit.

"Just the rest of the week, I'm afraid; the same goes for Billy; he's here too," said Tyler.

"Billy Desmond? Huh, where you go, he does too, right?" said Mr Nesbit.

"That's right. Listen, why don't you join us for a drink?" said Tyler.

"Oh no, I couldn't impose. You have your family there; it's your celebration," said Mr Nesbit.

"Mr Nesbit, you survived the trenches in the last war, and I know that when the Minister of Defence tried to skim my father on what he was owed for the contract, you made sure he was paid in full. To us, you are family," said Tyler.

"Please join us, Mr Nesbit," said Alice from the table with a smile. Mr Nesbit smiled a bit, too.

"Well, alright then," said Mr Nesbit as he grabbed his drink and sat down at the table with everyone.

"Billy, looking good, dear boy," said Mr Nesbit as he shook hands with Billy.

"Thank you, sir, a little worse for wear, as you can see", said Billy.

"We've all survived worse, my boy. And you know, slings and scars are actually a great attraction for the ladies," said Mr Nesbit with a wink.

"I'll remember that, sir," said Billy.

"And stop calling me sir; I'm not your commanding officer. It's Old Boy to you," said Old Boy.

Everyone returned to chatting for a few more minutes.

Mr Andrew Nesbit was a commissioned officer in the last war; he was in the trenches, leading his men into battle against the machine guns and across No Man's Land. The experience left him with some trauma, but he tried to recover by joining the construction efforts for a time in France. When the next war hit, Mr Nesbit was told twice that he wasn't fit for active duty, once because he was overage and a second because of his recurring trauma. Refusing to be stuck in an office in London, reading casualty reports and writing letters to soldier's families, Mr Nesbit signed up with the Home Guard in Millstone. The nickname Old Boy came from his age, but he didn't let that stop him from doing his bit.

During the conversation, Alice glanced at the bar and couldn't help noticing a young private and his friend looking across at their table; their faces were bland and without emotion. A cold chill went down Alice's spine.

Tyler then tapped on his glass to get everyone's attention as he stood up.

"Everyone, I have something I'd like to say," said Tyler.

"First of all, I'd like to thank my loving family for the welcome home they've given me. It's been an amazing day out and one to remember. I know that deep down...I hurt a lot of you when I signed up for the army, and I do apologise. Unfortunately, I will be heading back at the end of the week. For what it's worth, I really wish I could stay," said Tyler.

"But, before I head back, there's something that I really need to do, something I should've done a long time ago," said Tyler as he turned to Veronica, sitting next to him.

"Veronica, when we first met, I saw you walking down the street outside, and I said to myself, "There's no way I can ever talk to her; she's just too beautiful". Then you came to talk to me, and I was a gibbering idiot," said Tyler as Veronica laughed a bit.

"Then we courted, fell in love, and I know that I broke your heart when I left. But I consider it true love that you held out hope for my return and never found another man," said Tyler.

"I may have come close", Veronica teased.

"Which is why there's something I need to do. Something that I've discussed with my friend Billy and my father shortly before we went out this morning," said Tyler, suddenly getting down on one knee.

Everyone was surprised as Tyler pulled out an engagement ring; Veronica gasped quietly as she knew what it meant.

"Veronica Fox, will you consent to becoming my wife?" asked Tyler.

Everyone in the pub was quiet as they awaited an answer.

"Oh my stars, it's beautiful," said Veronica.

"Yes, yes I will!" said Veronica as Tyler's face lit up. He placed the ring on Veronica's finger, and it fit perfectly. They kissed, and the pub erupted into loud cheers.

The family started hugging Tyler and Veronica with happiness and some relief, but once again, Alice looked over at the bar and saw the private staring at Tyler again. This time, he was shaking his head and making a face as though he was disgusted.

That cold chill appeared again in Alice's spine.

"Well, I say this calls for another round," said Jack.

"I'll get it," said Tyler, getting up and heading for the bar.

Alice watched the private turn his head to follow Tyler as he did.

"You okay, Alice?" asked Lucy.

"That man at the other end of the bar, the private, keeps staring at Tyler. I've got a strange feeling about him," said Alice.

"Maybe you should tell Tyler," said Lucy.

"Yeah, yeah, you're right. I'll help Tyler with the drinks," Alice said the last bit to everyone as she got up and went to the bar.

"Hey, sis, you'll soon be calling Veronica that, won't you?" said Tyler.

"Yeah, I guess so," said Alice.

"So what's up? You're a little young to be drinking beer," Tyler jested.

"That private at the end of the bar, he's been staring at you for a while. And when you proposed to Veronica just now, I saw him shaking his head and acting disgusted," said Alice.

"Oh, did he now? Well, thank you for telling me, sis; I'll go and have a word with him," said Tyler.

"Be careful", said Alice.

"I will", said Tyler as he approached the private, who didn't even acknowledge his presence.

"Hey there, good to meet another fellow soldier here," said Tyler.

The private didn't respond, and neither did his friend.

"So you guys are on leave too, or are you AWOL? If that's the case, then Mum's the word," said Tyler, trying to make a joke, but neither one responded.

"Okay, do you have a problem with my proposal?" asked Tyler.

57

"Of course not; it couldn't have happened to a nicer girl. It's just a shame she's got hitched to the likes of you," said the private.

"What's that supposed to mean?" asked Tyler.

"She's the kind of girl that deserves love, care and affection. And none of that can come from a guy who thinks he can keep secrets and step over whoever he wants if they're in the way," said the private.

"Just who do you think you are?" asked Tyler.

The private got up from his seat and stood in front of him.

"My name is Wesley Dormer. I'm an acquaintance and good friend of one of your squad members, or should I say a former squad member? Andy Walker," said Wesley.

"I see; well, you have my condolences. Andy was a good man and didn't deserve a death like the one he got," said Tyler.

"Oh, to hell with your false pity! We all know that what you told the Generals is bullshit! You really expected us to believe that a grenade killed him? Well, we know better," said Wesley.

"That's what happened, and I'm sorry it did. If I could've helped him, then I would have, but his injuries were too great," said Tyler.

"So which one do you think is less important to you, the fact that you left his body behind for the

Nazis or the fact that your report is bullshit because you murdered him?!" said Wesley as several people in the bar gasped.

"Hey, don't talk to my brother like that, he's a hero!" said Alice.

"It's got nothing to do with you, half pint; stay out of it!" said Wesley.

"Hey, don't you talk to my sister like that!" said Tyler.

"Or what, come on, what will you do, lug me one in the throat?" asked Wesley as Tyler stood there.

"Just as I thought, people like you make me sick. Because you, Tyler Sherlock, are nothing more than a liar (he shoves Tyler) and a traitor! (he shoves Tyler again)" said Wesley.

"Leave him alone!" said Alice, shoving Wesley a bit. He then raised his hand and slapped her in the face.

Tyler punched Wesley and tackled him to the floor; the two of them started fighting like school boys in the playground. The second private got up and grabbed Tyler, trying to get him in a headlock, but Billy appeared and shoulder-tacked the guy to the side with his good arm, freeing Tyler as he went back to fighting Wesley. The private swung for Billy, who dodged both hits and delivered one back that knocked him to the ground. Tyler was about to punch Wesley again, but he heard Alice call out and stopped himself.

"You're not worth it. Don't touch my sister again!" said Tyler as he got up and went over to Alice.

Wesley then picked himself up, grabbed a glass from a table and went for Tyler again.

"Tyler!" said Alice as Old Boy suddenly grabbed Wesley's arm and delivered a punch that sent him to the floor.

"Okay, you two have had way too much to drink; it's time to go", said Mr Prosser as he picked up one of the privates.

"Yeah, time to sling your hook, fellas," said Tim as he picked up Wesley. He and Mr Prosser led them to the door.

"You think it's over; it's never going to be over. You won't get away with it; everyone will know the truth about Andy. You'll regret what you did!" shouted Wesley as he was dragged outside.

The pub was now very quiet, the atmosphere was ruined, and everyone was left wondering.

What had just happened?

The Sherlock Household, Evening, 9:00 pm

Everyone returned to the Sherlock house, and Jasper placed a call to Doctor Arthur, an ex-medic from the last war who now spends his days making house calls and tending to patients in surgery. He came round reasonably quick and looked over Alice's bruise and even a cut to Tyler's lip, a lucky swing from Wesley.

"Well, your lip will recover gradually, Tyler. But I'm afraid this bruise is going to last a while, young Alice. Take some of this Arnica liquid and spread it on the bruise three times a day," said Doctor Arthur.

"Thank you, Doctor" said Alice.

"No problem, it was brave of you to stand up for your brother. That's what the bruise should signify: bravery," said Doctor Arthur as Alice smiled.

"Thank you, Arthur. What is it we owe you?" said Jack.

"Oh please, Jack, I couldn't take your money. If Alice and Lucy hadn't found out who was using my key to steal medicine from the surgery, I would have lost my job and my licence," said Doctor Arthur.

"It's my pleasure to help out. Just try to avoid any more schoolboy brawls, eh Tyler," said Doctor Arthur.

"Sure thing, Doctor," said Tyler.

"I bid you all good evening," said Doctor Arthur as Jasper showed him the door.

"You okay, Alice?" asked Lucy.

"Well, it still hurts" replied Alice.

"I'm sorry, Alice, it's my fault. I shouldn't have confronted that guy," said Tyler.

"I'm the one who pointed him out, so it's my fault," said Alice.

"It's neither of your fault. Something tells me that he would've found a way to cause trouble, whether or not you noticed him," said Billy.

"I can't believe he had the gall to say such things in public. Why was he accusing you of murder, Tyler?" said Jack.

"All I can tell you, father, is its baseless lies. Me and I saw what happened to Andy. We tried our best to help him, but there was nothing we could do," said Tyler.

"Should we call the police about him?" asked Mavis.

"No, don't trouble yourself, mother. He was drunk and probably let his emotions for Andy get the best of him. Once he's sobered up, he'll realise his mistake," said Tyler.

"You think of too much good in people, son," said Mavis.

"There's plenty to be found, mother, out there somewhere," said Tyler.

"I hope my schoolboy brawl hasn't changed your mind about me, Veronica," said Tyler.

"Of course not, fiancée," said Veronica.

"Well, everyone, I think it's time to call it a night," said Jack.

"Yeah, I should be getting home; my Mum will start to worry. I'll see you for school tomorrow," said Lucy.

"I'll be there," said Alice as she and Lucy hugged.

"Are you sure about walking home by yourself, Lucy? It's very dark out there," said Mavis.

"I can walk her home. I need to stretch myself after that tackle anyway," said Billy.

"Good man, Billy," said Jack as Billy left the house with Lucy.

"I should be getting home too; I have to be ready for work tomorrow," said Veronica.

"I can walk you back," said Tyler.

"Are you sure after what happened?" asked Veronica.

"Nothing can keep me away from my fiancée," said Tyler.

"Tyler, before you go, will you help me to bed?" said Alice.

"A couple of minutes?" asked Tyler.

"Of course," said Veronica as Tyler led Alice upstairs to her room.

After a short while, Alice rubbed some of the Arnica on her bruise and ensured she wasn't sleeping on that side of her face. Tyler read more of the

Sherlock book chapters, and she was out like a light. Tyler stroked Alice's head, still feeling bad for what had happened to her.

He kissed her forehead and quietly left the room. As the door closed, Alice woke up slightly. She was still thinking about what had happened in the pub, and a worrying feeling passed though her.

Was Wesley really drunk enough that he didn't know what he was saying, or was there some frightening truth to his words?

Chapter 6

A Stab in the Dark

Millstone on Sea, Evening, 9:20 pm.

Tyler walks the streets with Veronica to her home, telling her the story of what happened to Andy in the field.

"And so I grabbed Billy and tackled him through the door just as the grenade went off. I tried to warn Andy, but I wasn't quick enough," said Tyler.

"I can still see him in my head. He was so frail; we told him to try and stay awake, but he couldn't even open his eyes. You know, I've thought that maybe there was a chance I could've reached him, I could've saved him," said Tyler.

"Then you might've been the one killed, or Billy" said Veronica.

"Yeah, I guess you're right," said Tyler.

"The worst part was leaving him there; we didn't want to; we wanted to bring him back, have him sent home and give him a dignified service. But the Nazis were coming back, and we didn't have the time; we had to get the prisoners out of there," said Tyler.

"Tyler, from what you've told me, it wasn't your fault. You tried your best; that's all anyone can do," said Veronica.

"Veronica, can I ask you a question?" asked Tyler.

"I thought you already had", said Veronica, showing the ring.

"Yes, no, I mean a different question," said Tyler.

"Of course," said Veronica.

"What if I didn't want to go back to the front? What if I wanted to hand in my resignation and come home properly?" asked Tyler.

"I thought they only allowed that if you're too injured to go back?" asked Veronica.

"Even so, what would you say to it?" asked Tyler.

"Well, it would be a great relief to me and your family, knowing that they won't soon get a letter saying you'd been killed in action. But it would still have to be your decision," said Veronica.

"I've seen a lot out there, Veronica; I've watched people killed, all for a stretch of land. War is hell; out there is hell," said Tyler.

"So yeah, maybe I can leave that part of it behind. Perhaps I can join with the Home Guard and patrol the town for parachutists and spies. It'd be a low-risk job on the home turf, and I'd still be doing my bit," said Tyler.

"Tyler, whatever you decide, I'll stand by you, and I'll love you forever," said Veronica as she and Tyler kissed.

They both kept walking and came up to the cinema.

"Hey, how about seeing if you can score us some movie tickets?" asked Tyler.

"I told you I have to be at work in the morning," said Veronica.

"For tomorrow, I meant when you get off work. Isn't that film you want to see, what is it, The Wizard of Oz showing?" said Tyler.

"Well, it is said to be full of colour and magic," said Veronica.

"Go on, I'll wait here," said Tyler as Veronica smiled and kissed his cheek, then raced over to the ticket booth.

Tyler held back and approached the side of the cinema, standing next to the entrance to an alleyway down the side. He looked around before pulling a letter out of his coat pocket; he read it and sighed; it was something that gave him relief or worry.

Tyler then heard a noise from behind him and turned around to look.

"ARGH!" Tyler was suddenly stabbed with a knife.

Whoever was holding the knife pulled it out of Tyler as he looked up and said, "You!" Then the figure plunged the knife into him again, closer to his chest. He reached into Tyler's pocket and pulled out the letter.

"No," said Tyler as the figure pulled out the knife.

Tyler stumbled back as Veronica looked in his direction.

"Tyler?" said Veronica as Tyler collapsed to the ground.

"TYLER!" screamed Veronica as she ran over to him.

A policeman across the road saw what was happening and caught sight of the figure in the alley.

"Oi!" he shouted while blowing his whistle, then took off after him.

Veronica took off her coat and tried using it to stop the bleeding, but Tyler was bleeding a lot. Other police officers came to help with the pursuit, and members of the Home Guard came with first aid kits to help Tyler.

But at one point, he stopped breathing.

Millstone on Sea Hospital, Evening, 10:30 pm

What was supposed to be a fun family outing for the Sherlocks had gone from a day of joy to a night of terror. Tyler was rushed to hospital as soon as he was stable enough to be moved, and he was sent into surgery immediately after arriving. The police sent a constable to inform the Sherlocks about what had happened. The household was awoken, and everyone raced to the hospital. They ran into Billy, who was just coming back from dropping Lucy off at home; her Mum liked to talk, which was why it took him a while to get back. He was shocked to hear what had happened and went with the family to the hospital. Veronica was already there; she went with the ambulance when they collected Tyler.

Nearly an hour later, the Sherlocks were still in the reception area, anxiously awaiting news of Tyler's condition. The same constable that informed them was eventually sent to collect Lucy, per Jack's instructions, knowing that Alice needed her friend during this trying time.

Lucy arrived not twenty minutes later.

"Alice!" said Lucy as she ran over and hugged her.

"The constable told me Tyler was in the hospital, but he wouldn't say why," said Lucy.

"Tyler was walking Veronica home....she stopped to buy some tickets for the cinema....and someone came out of the alley and stabbed Tyler!" said Alice as she started to break down crying; Lucy kept hugging her.

She wasn't the only one; everyone there shared a series of tears, all of them thinking of Tyler and trying to stay positive, but it was hard. Even harder than praying he wouldn't die in the war, far away from them.

Finally, a doctor came through a set of doors and approached them.

"The Sherlocks?" asked the Doctor as everyone got up.

"That's us, how is he, Doctor?" said Jack.

"Well, I have good news and bad news," said the Doctor.

"Give us the good news, Doctor, please," said Mavis.

"The good news is that Tyler is a very, very lucky man. Both stabs missed hitting any vital organs entirely, which gives him a strong chance of recovery," said the Doctor.

Everyone started breathing sighs of relief.

"Wait, what's the bad news?" asked Billy.

"The bad news is that Tyler's still bleeding inside; it's slow, but it's happening. We need to find the source of the bleeding and patch it up before we stitch the wounds themselves," said the Doctor.

"Can we see him?" asked Alice.

"I'm afraid that's not advisable; we've had to put Tyler in a heavily sedated coma. The next few days will determine whether or not he'll survive," said the Doctor.

"But you just said he has a strong chance of recovery," said Jack.

"I said he has a strong chance because his organs are still intact, and that's true. But if we can't find where the bleeding is coming from and stop it…his chance will start dwindling," said the Doctor.

Everyone's worries resurfaced with new fears.

"Doctor, is there no way you can at least permit Alice to see her brother, even just for a minute? She deserves to see him, even if he can't talk back," pleaded Mavis as the Doctor thought for a moment.

"Okay, I'll see what I can do," said the Doctor as he turned and left.

"Thanks, Mum," said Alice.

"Of course, dear," said Mavis as they hugged.

Alice then turned to Veronica and held her hand.

"I know that'll sound silly, but are you okay, Veronica?" said Alice.

"I'm not, to be honest with you, Alice. I was only inches away from him. I'd left him mere seconds ago, and when I turned back, he was clasping his chest and fell to the ground," said Veronica.

"Did they find who did it?" asked Alice.

"Some policemen chased a figure into the alley, but they lost sight of him," said Veronica.

"Did you see who it was?" asked Alice.

"No, it was too dark, and I was too far away," said Veronica.

"You know, I heard the same policemen talking before I got into the ambulance with Tyler. They were saying it could be a robbery gone wrong," said Veronica.

"Was anything taken?" asked Alice.

"That's the thing. When I got into the ambulance, I checked Tyler's pockets; he still had his wallet and the watch his Dad gave him before he left for the front," said Veronica.

"Maybe whoever did this meant to take the stuff when he was down, but you interrupted him; you saved Tyler's life," said Alice.

"Yeah, I hope so," said Veronica.

"Alice darling, I think that's enough of the questions. Veronica's been through a lot, same as the rest of us," said Mavis.

"Sorry, Mum," said Alice.

"I know you want answers; we all do. But I think it's best to leave this to the police; it's not one of your cases, darling," said Mavis.

Alice gave a small smile and got up; Mavis tried to comfort Veronica while Lucy pulled Alice to the side.

"You don't think it was a robbery, do you?" asked Lucy.

"Tyler is a soldier, trained in combat, and I know for a fact it includes learning what to do when taken by surprise. And you heard Veronica; he still had his watch and wallet on him," said Alice.

"So you think there's more to this?" asked Lucy.

"I don't know, what if I'm getting all worked up about it? What if Mum's right? This isn't one of my cases; maybe it really was a robbery gone poorly, and I just think it's a mystery because of a feeling I get," said Alice.

"And what if you're right, and someone actually did this to Tyler? The robbery may have been a convincing cover if Veronica hadn't surprised the attacker," said Lucy.

"Are you really going to leave this to the police if that's the case?" asked Lucy.

Alice didn't answer; she was deep in thought.

The doctor then came back through the doors.

"I can allow Tyler's sister five minutes; that's the best I can do," said the Doctor.

"Go on, Alice, we'll wait here," said Mavis as Alice followed the doctor to Tyler's room.

The doctor showed Alice into the room; she felt some nausea, seeing Tyler in bed with a breathing mask on his face.

"I'll be back in five minutes," said the Doctor as he left the room.

Alice slowly approached Tyler's bedside.

"I can't leave you alone for a moment, can I?" said Alice, trying to be funny, but it didn't work.

"It's not fair. We only just got you back, and now we feel like we're losing you all over again," said Alice as she held Tyler's hand.

"The police say that a mugger did this; it was just some random thief that went wrong. But I don't believe it, not for a minute. If that was the case, the mugger would be the injured one, not you," said Alice, fighting back her tears.

"That means someone did this to you, whether it was to wound or kill you, I don't know," said Alice.

"But I promise you, Tyler, I will do whatever it takes to find out who did this, and I will make sure they do justice," said Alice.

"I won't let you down, brother, just…stay alive…for me….for all of us", said Alice as tears trickled down her face.

The doctor came back and returned Alice to her family; everyone went home shortly afterwards.

But Alice had made a promise to Tyler, and she intended to keep it.

Chapter 7

A Guiding Hand

The Sherlock Household, next morning, 9:00 am

The house was quiet when everyone got home; they all went straight to bed shortly after, but no one slept that night. Everyone was still quite tired the next morning, so they tried to have some lie-ins before getting up. Jasper prepared breakfast when everyone was ready, but it was still silent around the table; no one felt like talking; their minds were too wiped out. At one point, the phone rang, and Jack answered. It was from the school; they'd heard about Tyler and wanted to give Alice the day off to rest and recuperate, but they still expected her in tomorrow. Jack informed Alice, who wasn't too happy with it, not that she said anything besides "Ok".

After breakfast was finished, the doorbell rang, and Jasper answered it.

"It's Miss Porter for you, Miss Alice," said Jasper as Alice went to the front door.

"Hey Alice," said Lucy.

"Hey, Lucy," said Alice.

"I thought it might be good to walk to school with you. Why aren't you dressed yet? Classes start soon," said Lucy.

"I'm not going to school today; they just called and gave me the day off because of what happened to Tyler," said Alice.

"And, you're okay with that?" asked Lucy.

"Not really. I was already moping around the house this morning, and we've barely even spoken to each other. Now, my one distraction decided to act in my best interest," said Alice.

"Well, I wish I could stay, but they didn't give me the day off," said Lucy.

"It's okay, Lucy, you go. It's just for today; they'll be expecting me back tomorrow," said Alice.

"Okay, well, I'll come by afterwards to see how you are, and maybe we can talk about how we're going to help Tyler," said Lucy.

"I appreciate that, Lucy, but I wouldn't blame you if you didn't want to be a part of it. This is a real case we're entering, not the ones we're used to," said Alice.

"Hey, I've been your partner for two years. As you said when we started this, you're Sherlock Holmes, and I'm Doctor John Watson. You can't have one without the other," said Lucy.

"Thank you, Lucy," said Alice as she and Lucy hugged.

"Take care now, and try to find a distraction," said Lucy as she left.

"I'll try," said Alice as she waved Lucy off and closed the door.

After a few minutes, Alice put her coat and shoes on and told Jasper that if anyone asked where she was, she'd sit outside for a bit to clear her head, and then she left by the front door.

Alice had found a nice spot by the cliffs where they lived, but not too close to the edge. She sat there and stared at the view; it sometimes helped her think, and she really needed the help. Alice thought about her promise to Tyler. She wanted so much to see it, but a troubling thought had cropped up in her mind.

"Where am I supposed to start?" Alice said to herself.

"Sometimes the most logical place to start is right at the beginning," said a voice from the side.

Alice slowly turned her head and couldn't believe it.

Sitting next to her, wearing a brown cape deerstalker hat and holding a pipe, was Sherlock Holmes.

"Mr Holmes?" said Alice.

"Not really. I mean, I am Sherlock Holmes, but not really here, elsewhere," said Sherlock.

"What?" asked Alice, confused.

"I'm Sherlock Holmes, but I'm only up here (he points at Alice's head). Not the most logical solution, but it is what it is," said Sherlock.

"So wait, how am I seeing you right now?" asked Alice.

"I don't know. I'm feeling emotionally stressed, worrying about your brother, and wondering if you can help him. That and your rather obsessive fan base about me," said Sherlock.

"I'm not an "obsessive" fan. I just really like reading about you; your adventures with Watson are amazing," said Alice.

"You sleep at night while hugging one of my books," said Sherlock.

"I like to read a few pages before I sleep. Sometimes, I doze off. And any hugging you, I mean the book, is purely to do with the deep sleep state," said Alice.

"Quite an intelligent head on your shoulders; it's nice to see," said Sherlock.

"So, why am I seeing you now?" asked Alice.

"Well, I thought it was obvious. You're about to take on your first real case, nothing like the dog finding or jewel recovery you're used to," said Sherlock.

"And since you just asked about where to start, the answer to your question is that you're hoping I can give you some advice," said Sherlock.

"I've read your stories for a long time, Mr Holmes, and I've always wanted to be like you. But there's no way I can ever do the things you and Watson have done," said Alice.

"It's not all intelligence and deduction, Alice. Sometimes you require brawn, calm minds, a little brute strength and the occasional use of Watson's revolver, which happens more often than not," said Sherlock.

"But you guys are legends. You've gone up against serial killers, master thieves, international crime rings and scandals in other countries," said Alice.

"I'm quite sure that Watson exaggerates his writings a bit. But people seem to enjoy them, and it's more work for us," said Sherlock.

"And the fact you can tell everything about a person just by looking at them, there's no way I can ever do that," said Alice.

"That doesn't mean it's a popular characteristic. Besides, you already have your deduction skills; you never miss a detail, which is important," said Sherlock.

"Am I doing the right thing, Mr Holmes? Taking on a case like this to find out who attacked my brother? Maybe I should leave it to the police after all," said Alice.

"Alice, do you think Lestrade could have solved all those cases himself? I mean, probably, but he would've done it all wrong. Sometimes the law needs that bit of help from Watson and me, not to show them up, but to provide an intellectual hand," said Sherlock.

"And it's not like you're doing it for selfish reasons; it's to help your family," said Sherlock.

"But, am I ready for something of this scale?" asked Alice.

"Only you can answer that question," said Sherlock.

"Then I'm going to do it; I'll keep my promise to Tyler," said Alice.

"And I'm taking your advice too, start at the beginning. That soldier Wesley, who picked a fight with Tyler, sounded like he knew stuff, and there's the alley where Tyler's attacker disappeared," said Alice.

"You see, you can do anything if you put your mind to it," said Sherlock.

"But how am I going to start investigating on my own? Lucy is my partner, but she's in school right now," said Alice.

"Well, you know, Alice, sometimes there's a point where we have to ask Lestrade for help. A man of rather simple tastes and not that big of imagination but a loyal officer and ally that you may well need on your side," said, Sherlock.

"Yeah, I think I get what you're saying," said Alice.

"Then the game is afoot, Alice," said Sherlock as Alice looked back and saw he'd disappeared.

Alice couldn't believe what had just happened, but her thoughts turned to Sherlock's advice, and she quickly came up with who to ask for help.

"Billy," said Alice.

Billy's Cave, Morning, 9:20 am.

Alice made her way down to the beach below her home and took a left, following the cliffs until she came to an opening that led into a sizable cavern. This was Billy's cave; he found it a number of years ago when he and Tyler were in their student years. Since then, Billy began moving bits and pieces into the cave: chairs, a radio with an antenna, some food packets, water bottles, plenty of books and even a workshop where he tinkered with small devices and appliances. This cave became something of a secret hideaway, a place Billy could go to for some peace and quiet. He eventually shared its location with Tyler on the promise he'd keep it a secret, but Tyler couldn't help telling Alice about it.

Alice carefully crossed the gap between the cave and the beach, balancing on some stepping stones and trying not to fall into the water. That happened to her once; her Mum wasn't very pleased. Alice made it to the other side and slowly entered the cave; she saw Billy tinkering at his workshop and started to approach him.

"Hey Alice," said Billy, without turning around.

"How did you know it was me?" asked Alice.

"Someone with your soft footsteps, plus being the only one Tyler told about this place, lucky guess," said Billy.

"I figured you'd be here, your special cave," said Alice.

"Yeah, I half expected to find the cave flooded or everything here had rusted and rotted away. It's a miracle it's all still in good condition," said Billy.

"Actually, we may have had something to do with it. Me, Dad, Mum, and even Jasper have tried to look after the place. It meant I had to reveal its existence to them, but we kept things working and moved it all on the days the tide would come in," said Alice.

"Thank you, Alice, I appreciate it," said Billy.

"So, did you come by just to check on me?" asked Billy.

"Actually, no, I'm here to ask for your help," said Alice.

"With what?" asked Billy.

"I'm going to investigate what happened to Tyler. I'd like you to join me and Lucy," said Alice.

"You're going to investigate? Have you been appointed Special Constable while I've been in this cave?" asked Billy.

"No, look, Billy, the police want to label the attack as a failed robbery. You know as well as I do

Tyler would've never let that happen to him. That means whoever did it meant to kill him," said Alice.

"Alice, you've been reading Sherlock Holmes for too long. You've become paranoid, conspiratorial; nothing going on here requires deduction; it's just a case of wrong place, wrong time," said Billy.

"How can you say that after what happened? I saw the bandaged wounds on Tyler, one stab maybe to get away, but then in his chest? He was supposed to die, and the attacker knew that," said Alice.

"Alice, just stop it!" said Billy in a fierce tone.

"This isn't a game; this is real life, and I'm fully aware of Tyler's condition. Just leave this alone and let the police handle it," said Billy.

"Now please go, Alice. I'm very busy, and if I hear anything more about you investigating, I'll tell your mother," said Billy.

Alice couldn't believe what she was hearing. Was this really Billy talking? How could he not want to find out who attacked his best friend? Alice turned and started to leave the cave, but she stopped and turned back for a moment.

"You know, if the roles were reversed and it was you in hospital with those wounds, Tyler would do whatever it took to find the person responsible. Because he told me that brothers, blood-related or not, always have each other's backs....but I guess he was wrong," said Alice as she left the cave.

Billy didn't say anything; he just remained silent, contemplating what Alice had said.

It may have been hurtful, but it was true.

Chapter 8

The Investigation Begins

<u>Millstone on Sea Cinema, Morning, 10:00 am</u>

Alice had made her way into town, heading for the cinema. She kept stopping for people who offered their sympathy and wished Tyler well. Alice finally made it to the cinema and looked around the area for the alley that Veronica had mentioned. She then made her way into the alley, searching for clues that might help identify the attacker. A needle in a haystack, but she had to try.

Alice had only been looking for a couple of minutes when she turned around and found two homeless people blocking the way out.

"Spare something?" asked one of the homeless.

Alice didn't have any hate or disgust for homeless people, so she reached into her pocket, pulled out some change, and then handed it to him.

"Most kind young lady," said the homeless man as he started to leave, but the other one stayed.

"Got something for me to do, sweetheart?" said the other homeless man.

"I'm sorry, that's all I have now," said Alice.

"Oh, don't give me that; you rich kids always have such tight pockets. Yeah, that's right, I know who you are; now, how about something more?" said the homeless man as he suddenly pulled a knife.

"What are you doing?" asked the first homeless man.

"Getting more than we're owed out of the rich snobs who cost me my job, now empty your pockets," said the second homeless man.

Alice looked scared, but she then dropped into a defensive stance.

"I must warn you, my brother and father have taught me a number of self-defence moves. You come near me, and you'll be sorry," said Alice.

"Kids are so cute, aren't they?" said the second homeless man as he started to approach Alice.

But his expression suddenly changed when he received a karate chop to the side of his shoulder; he fell unconscious on the ground and revealed the person standing behind him was Billy.

"I knew you'd come," said Alice.

"And I knew you wouldn't give up on this," said Billy.

The first homeless man was shaking a bit and dropped the change Alice had given him. She picked it up.

"Take it back; I'm so sorry. I didn't know he was going to do that; I'm not like him, I swear!" said the homeless man.

"It's okay; you're not going to be hurt. But, a question if that's okay?" said Alice.

"Um, what's the question?" asked the homeless man.

"Were you here last night, in this alley?" asked Alice.

"I was, yeah, I'm usually here most nights," said the homeless man.

"Did you see the attack that took place just at the entrance?" asked Alice.

"You mean with that soldier? Yeah, I saw it; the guy who stabbed him ran right past me, followed by a policeman. I just hid behind the bins; I didn't want to get involved," said the homeless man.

"Did you see anything that can help identify him?" asked Alice.

"I'm sorry, no, like I said, I tried to stay hidden so he wouldn't see me. But, actually, over by those bins, I saw him throw something like some crumpled-up paper," said the homeless man as Billy went to check.

He moved some of the bins and found a piece of crumpled-up paper. He opened it to find it had writing on it, but some were stained with red.

"This must be it," said Billy as Alice handed the change back to the homeless man.

"Take it, my good man, and thank you for your help," said Alice.

"God bless you, young miss; I hope you find what you're looking for. But be careful, I may not have seen his face, but his vicious attack on that soldier suggests he's done it before," said the homeless man.

"I'll be careful; you take care now," said Alice as the homeless man smiled and walked away.

Billy was trying to read what was on the paper.

"What does it say?" asked Alice.

"I can't really tell; most of it is obscured behind this red stain; I think it might be.....oh," said Billy.

Alice was about to ask what it was, but part of her already knew.

"It's blood, isn't it? Tyler's?" asked Alice.

"I think it might be. He must have had this in his coat when he was stabbed," said Billy.

"Can you figure out what it says?" asked Alice.

"Um, something, dragon, something, safe, something....." Billy seemed to stop mid-sentence.

"What, what does it say?" asked Alice.

"Nothing, um, I can't figure it out," said Billy as he handed the paper to Alice.

"Well, it's the one clue we've found so far. It's best we keep hold of it until we can decipher the contents," said Alice as she folded and pocketed the paper.

"You sure you don't want me to hold onto it?" asked Billy.

"No, it's okay. This may have been important to Tyler; I'd like to keep it close," said Alice.

"So, what's the next step?" asked Billy.

"Well, there's only one other thing I can think of, and that is to question the one person we've seen who had a motive for attacking Tyler", said Alice.

"Wesley, the private from last night's fight," said Billy.

"He seemed very convinced that Tyler had something to do with Andy's death, so much so that he was willing to step up and publicly accuse him," said Alice.

"I was there when Andy died, Alice. It was a tragic and unfortunate accident. If Tyler had saved him, he would have. But in that situation, he likely would've died too," said Billy.

"But even with your account, it's still enough that someone could be spinning stories and getting the wrong end of the stick," said Alice.

"So, we're going to question him now?" asked Billy.

"We are, but there's one problem. Where do we find him?" said Alice.

The Anchor Pub, Morning, 10:15 am

Alice and Billy went back to the George and Dragon pub; they questioned Mr Prosser and Tim about Wesley and where they could find him. Mr Prosser told them that Wesley was well known for being a troublemaker; his father sent him to the war to get him to be a man until he was discharged for misconduct. But he was also school friends with Andy; they were very close, and when Wesley heard about Andy dying, he refused to believe it was because he wasn't fast enough to avoid a grenade; he wanted answers. Tim then mentioned that Wesley only frequented two pubs, theirs and the Anchor, so Billy and Alice headed there to find him.

They went inside and quickly spotted Wesley sitting towards the back of the pub with some of his friends, one of them being the private Billy tackled during the fight.

As they tried to approach him, the barman stopped them.

"Hold on a minute, how old are you, young lady?" asked the barman.

"I'm twelve, sir" replied Alice.

"Sorry, can't let you in without an adult," said the barman.

"She's with me, it's okay," said Billy.

"And who are you, her suitor?" said the barman with slight sarcasm.

"He's my friend; we're looking for information about my brother, Tyler Sherlock," said Alice.

"Tyler....oh my goodness, you're Alice Sherlock, aren't you?" said the barman.

"We've never met, mostly because my pub is on the other side of town. But I've heard about you, Millstone's little investigator. Aren't you supposed to have a partner, though?" said the barman.

"Yeah, Lucy, she's in school at the moment," said Alice.

"My condolences for your brother; I hope he recovers," said the barman.

"Thank you," said Alice.

"Is there anything I can do to help?" asked the barman.

"We just have a couple of questions for Wesley," said Billy.

"Oh, okay, he's over there, table towards the back. But hey, I don't want any trouble," said the barman.

"There won't be any....I hope," Alice said the last bit quietly to herself as she and Billy approached Wesley at his table.

"So, you back for round two then?" asked Wesley.

"Not this time, we just want to talk to you, Wesley," said Billy.

"I've got nothing to say to either of you. If you've come expecting apologies, you're out of luck," said Wesley.

"We want to ask you some questions about Tyler," said Alice.

"Ah, of course, hero Tyler. The man they're willing to let get away with everything because he's some bootlicking stooge," said Wesley.

"Don't you talk about him like that! Ask the question, Alice," said Billy.

"Did you stab my brother?" asked Alice as Wesley's expression changed.

"Wait, what?" asked Wesley.

"Tyler was stabbed last night; he's in hospital in critical condition," said Billy.

"My god, I didn't know; I'm really sorry," said Wesley.

"Oh, so now you're showing remorse?!" asked Alice.

"Hey, it's not like that. I just wanted answers for what really happened to Andy; how am I supposed to get them if he's dead?" said Wesley.

"You were talking about that in the pub last night. What do you think really happened to Andy?" said Billy as Wesley got up and approached him, then pulled a letter out of his jacket pocket.

"Andy sent this to me shortly before he left for Yugoslavia; he wrote on the envelope that it was only to be opened in the event of his death. After hearing what happened, I opened it, and this is what it said," said Wesley as he read the letter

"To Wesley

If you're reading this, it means that I'm likely dead, killed in the line of duty or some other cause. I've been forced to keep a secret among the squad for the last couple of months. For your safety, I cannot divulge what it is on the chance this letter falls into the hands of the enemy or the Home Office. But suffice to say, I'm now part of a pact that means I cannot tell anyone this secret, but it's something big, something that could change our lives or destroy them. I've been trying to sow doubt with the others in the squad, trying to convince them that what we're doing is wrong. But my actions have caught Tyler Sherlock's attention; I fear that he may decide I'm too much of a liability and ensure I have an "accident" to safeguard the pact. You've always been a good friend to me, Wesley, so I'm now entrusting this to you. If anything should happen to me, try to find out what it was, whether I died defending my country or if my death was a suspicious one. If it was murder like I'm expecting, don't let Tyler Sherlock get away with it. Long live England. Andy Walker".

"That's bullshit! Andy wouldn't have written something like that!" said Billy.

"Can I see it?" asked Alice as Wesley handed the letter to her and she read it.

"It's all true, Billy, word for word," said Alice as Billy took the letter and read it too.

"That's Andy's handwriting," said Billy.

"So you see, I don't know what this secret or pact you guys have is. But I know it had Andy scared, and I refuse to believe that his death was an empty one," said Wesley.

"Well, you say you want answers, but maybe your need for revenge got to you, and that's when you stabbed Tyler," said Alice.

"Look, princess, it's justice I want, not revenge. And another thing, would I really be so stupid as to attack your brother only a while after we had a fight? Because it would be my door, and the police would be knocking on first," said Wesley.

"He has a point," said Billy.

"He does now. I think it's time for you both to move on. Unless it's time for round two with the one-armed bandit," said the private.

Billy suddenly removed his sling and showed his arm was much better.

"Or maybe we can make it more of a contest this time," said Billy.

"Hey, I said I don't want any trouble," said the barman.

"Relax, David, I think it's time for us to leave anyway," said Wesley as he and his friends gulped the rest of their drinks and headed for the exit, but Wesley turned back.

"You may not believe me, and I don't blame you, but I am sorry for your brother. I don't wish him dead; that's for the court to decide," said Wesley as he left the bar.

Alice and Billy left shortly after.

"You okay?" asked Billy.

"I was kind of hoping you'd punch him. But as much as I hate to admit it, he was right," said Alice.

"Yeah, he'd be the first visit from the police if he stabbed Tyler so soon after the fight," said Billy.

"What worries me is the contents of the letter. What's this pact that Andy mentioned?" said Alice.

"I have no idea; there's certainly no pact among us. I don't know why Andy would say that," said Billy.

"So, we're back to square one?" asked Billy.

"Not yet; there's still one more avenue to check," said Alice.

"And what's that?" asked Billy.

"By now, the police would have finished the preliminary examinations of Tyler's wounds, confirmed it with the doctor, taken statements and gathered what evidence they could find. And it should all be in a file at the police station," said Alice.

"What are you getting at?" asked Billy.

"I need to get into the police station and look at that file," said Alice.

"Oh my...Alice, I think you're taking things too far. That's close to breaking several laws, and if you're caught, they'll lock you up," said Billy.

"Well, that's why you'll have to make sure I don't get caught," said Alice.

"Alice, there may not be many policemen in the station, but there's still no way you can sneak past whoever is there. Besides, you don't even know where the file might be," said Billy.

"The Chief of Police would likely be reading it, so it should be in his office. And as for the police inside, we're going to have to get creative," said Alice.

"Oh, I'm going to regret this one day", said Billy as he and Alice headed for the police station.

Chapter 9

Police Evidence

Millstone on Sea Police Station, Noon, 12:00 pm

The police station wasn't too much to look at; it'd already been bombed and rebuilt during the last year. But now its manpower was diminished; only a handful of police constables, including the Chief Inspector and the Sergeant, worked there. Alice and Billy had the right idea of waiting for lunchtime when most of the constables would either still be on patrol or partaking in lunch. But they still had to get past the Chief and the Sergeant, who always made sure they were on duty should anyone need assistance.

Alice and Billy had to get creative if they wanted to see what was in the file about Tyler's attack.

Inside the waiting area, the Sergeant sat at the front desk, enjoying a cheese sandwich for his lunch. The Chief came out of his office at the end of the hallway to the right.

"How are things, Sergeant?" asked the Chief.

"All quiet, sir, nothing but the mice," said the Sergeant.

"Oh, don't get me started on the mice. Little pests, running all over the floor and nicking off with your chocolate biscuit after dropping it, " said the Chief.

"Did you finish looking through the file on Tyler Sherlock's attacker?" asked the Sergeant.

"I did, everything's in order. Once Doctor Arthur has delivered the preliminary medical exam, we can file it away and close the case," said the Chief.

"But sir, we haven't found the attacker yet," said the Sergeant.

"And it's likely we won't. Whoever this guy is knows that he tried to kill a soldier; he's no doubt got the Home Guard after him, and even if he skips town, he'll have the Army hunting him down," said the Chief.

"It's out of our hands now. All we can do is finish the paperwork, tell the family our findings and let nature take its course," said the Chief.

Suddenly, Billy came running into the station.

"Sergeant, I need your help!" said Billy.

"What's wrong, sir?" asked the Sergeant.

"I think I just spotted a Nazi in the alley down the street," said Billy.

"A Nazi? Are you sure, sir?" asked the Sergeant.

"I think so. His eyes were too close together, and he had a craggy jaw with a scar on his face," said Billy.

"I'll inform the Home Guard," said the Sergeant.

"What are you playing at, Sergeant? By the time they get down here, the Nazis could be long gone. We need to handle this ourselves," said the Chief.

"But there's only two of us, sir, and what if he's armed?" said the Sergeant.

"If it helps, I have experience with tackling Nazis," said Billy.

"That makes three of us, Sergeant. We're the police; how is it going to look to the public if we run off, blubbing to the Home Guard because we can't handle one Nazi?" said the Chief.

The Sergeant still wasn't sure, but he seemed to reluctantly agree with the idea.

"Take us to where you saw him", said the Chief as Billy led him and the Sergeant out of the station.

Seconds after they left, Alice snuck in the front and made her way to the Chief's office; she knew where it was after she and Lucy were once brought in for trespassing on private property. But the charge was dropped when it turned out the owner liked stealing jewellery from unsuspecting women.

Alice made it into the office and went over to the Chief's desk; the file was still there; she opened it and started looking through the paperwork. It seemed to be a series of statements from the family, nearby witnesses, and potential suspects, including Wesley.

But more papers were confirmed alibis; Wesley had one, so he was off the hook. Otherwise, it was evidence collection and accounting, but Alice wasn't finding anything she'd hoped would help.

"Damn it, there's nothing here," said Alice as her heart dropped when the door to the office opened.

Billy had led the Chief and Sergeant away from the station and brought them down to the first alley he saw. It led to a wide-open dead end.

"So where's this Nazi?" asked the Chief.

"He...was....here," said Billy.

It seemed his ruse was about to collapse.

"Wait a minute, sir. Something moved behind that bin there," said the Sergeant.

"You check it out," the Chief said to Billy.

"You've got the experience; we'll back you up," said the Sergeant.

Billy slowly approached the bin; he hadn't planned for this, so he had no idea what to expect. As he reached the bin and slowly moved it, a rat sprinted out from behind it.

"AHHH, a mouse, it's a mouse!" said the Chief.

"It's a rat, sir!" said the Sergeant.

"I don't care what it is, kill it, kill it, Sergeant!" said the Chief as he and the Sergeant were waving their nightsticks around, trying to hit the rat as it sprinted back and forth.

Billy held back, slightly bemused as to what he was witnessing.

Back at the office, the door opened. Alice's heart dropped, but she felt a slight relief for a moment when it turned out to be Doctor Arthur.

"Alice, what in blazes are you doing in here?" asked Doctor Arthur.

"Please, Doctor, I can explain," said Alice.

"I think you'd better," said Doctor Arthur.

"I'm not trying to do anything illegal, not really. I'm trying to find out who attempted to kill Tyler," said Alice.

"Alice, I know you want answers, but sneaking into a police station and looking at confidential files isn't the way. If you get caught, you'll be charged with trespassing, for real this time," said Doctor Arthur.

"Doctor, please understand. I refuse to believe that this was because some thief wanted his wallet. I think someone actually tried to kill my brother, and I have to get to the truth before they try again," said Alice.

"I only just got my brother back; I can't lose him again, especially not like this. Please, Doctor, don't tell on me, help me, please!" begged Alice.

Unlike most people, Doctor Arthur was a man of principles and followed the law. But he knew that it was usually right when Alice had a hunch.

"If this was anyone else, I'd raise the alarm. But I respect what you're doing, and since you and Lucy are the reason I still have a job, I'll do what I can," said Doctor Arthur.

"Well, I need something to prove that Tyler's attack was attempted murder, but everything in this file is pointing towards a failed robbery", said Alice.

"Maybe not everything. I just finished the preliminary exam on Tyler's wounds and was going to give it to the Chief. But since he's indisposed, you'll have to do it," said Doctor Arthur as he approached the desk and showed Alice the papers he was carrying.

"I'm sorry for what you're about to see, but I needed these pictures to work with. If it's a robbery, most thieves tend to use small knives or shivs. Granted, those only exist in prison, but there are some out here, too," said Doctor Arthur.

"However, I remembered seeing these types of wounds during my time in the medical corps. Tyler was stabbed with an Army Issue Bayonet," said Doctor Arthur.

"A bayonet?" asked Alice.

"Yes, long, sharp and capable of puncturing a number of organs in one strike," said Doctor Arthur as he realised what he'd just said.

"Um, sorry, Alice, I shouldn't have said that" said Doctor Arthur.

"No, it's okay. You've found the first real evidence that what happened to Tyler wasn't an accident. Someone WAS trying to kill him," said Alice.

"And that's a good thing?" asked Doctor Arthur.

"It means that the police are wrong. This wasn't some random thief who wanted money; it was premeditated. My brother was targeted, and you have the proof. Doctor, you're amazing!" said Alice as she hugged Doctor Arthur.

"Oh, it's...my pleasure, Alice," said Doctor Arthur.

"Now, I best get you out of here before the Chief comes back," said Doctor Arthur as he led Alice out of the office.

Just as they headed for the front entrance, they caught the Chief and the Sergeant as they were returning with Billy. They both looked out of breath.

"Are....are you sure you got it, Sergeant?" asked the Chief.

"Fairly sure....sir. Not unless it has a convincing body double," said the Sergeant.

"Doctor Arthur," said the Chief.

"Just bringing the preliminary exam; sorry it took so long. I've left it on your desk," said Doctor Arthur.

"Oh, good. And Alice Sherlock, what brings you here?" asked the Chief.

"I...I wanted to ask if you have any information on who attacked my brother. My parents would really like things to start making sense, but when I came here, no one was in, so I decided to wait," said Alice.

"Well, you can tell your parents that we have no choice but to close the case. No new evidence has come up, so we don't have anything to go on. But we're confident it was simply a thief who went too far," said the Chief.

"Thank you, Chief; I'll be sure to let them know," said Alice.

"Again, I'm really sorry about the Nazi that turned out to be a...rat," said Billy.

"No, no, sir. You did the right thing by telling us, but maybe next time...try to get a better look," said the Sergeant.

"Well, I must be off. I have patients waiting; good day, gents, Alice," said Doctor Arthur as he left the station.

"If you'll excuse us, Alice, I think the Sergeant and I need some time to catch our breath," said the Chief.

"Come on, Alice, I'll walk you home," said Billy as Alice followed him out of the station.

They walked a little way before stopping to talk.

"So, did you find anything?" asked Billy.

"I found a gold mine," said Alice.

"You didn't say you were going to dig a tunnel", Billy teased.

"I didn't find much, but Doctor Arthur did. His exam shows the knife that stabbed Tyler was actually a bayonet," said Alice.

"You're kidding," said Billy.

"I'm not; he was in the medical corps long enough to know what bayonet wounds looked like. Billy, you know what this means?" said Alice.

"A soldier nearly killed Tyler," said Billy.

"Exactly," said Alice.

"Okay, so what's the next step?" said Billy.

"I think now we should wait until school's finished, then we can bring Lucy up to speed and-" Alice stopped when the all too familiar sound of the air raid siren began ringing out.

"Oh no, here they come again. We're not far from your house, come on," said Billy as he took Alice's hand, and the two of them ran through the streets back to the Sherlock house.

They made it back pretty quickly as Jack, Mavis, and Jasper opened the shelter they had built in their basement, and the door was on the outside.

Mavis was looking for Alice as she ran up the pathway with Billy.

"There you are; where have you been? I've been worried sick!" said Mavis.

"I..just went for a walk with Billy," said Alice.

"Well, never mind that now, everyone is in the shelter!" said Jack as everyone ran down the stairs into the basement. Jasper then followed as he closed and locked the door.

Time in the shelters wasn't really for talking; everyone mostly sat quietly and occasionally gasped after hearing a plane go over or the ground rumble as something heavy was dropped, most likely a bomb.

It was only one of many nerve-wracking waits experienced by families all over the country.

Sherlock Household, Afternoon, 3:20 pm

Roughly three hours passed before the all-clear sounded that it was safe for everyone to emerge from their shelters and bunkers. Billy headed into town to find out what the damage was, and shortly after he left, Lucy suddenly appeared along the pathway. She always came to check if Alice was okay and said she'd do the same for Lucy. Alice took Lucy to her room and started filling her in on everything she and Billy had learned.

"A soldier?" asked Lucy.

"That's what Doctor Arthur reckons; it's the only way to explain the bayonet wounds," said Alice.

"But, don't certain members of the Home Guard use bayonets? I've seen a few walking around with them," said Lucy.

"Well, I didn't say the soldier was from the front lines," said Alice.

"It still doesn't make sense, though. Why would someone want to kill Tyler? He's one of the nicest guys I know," said Lucy.

"I think the answer to that question, at least a part of it, may lie in this letter," said Alice as she pulled out the letter from the alley and handed it to Lucy.

"Is this Tyler's blood?" asked Lucy.

Alice didn't answer.

"I'm sorry," said Lucy.

"I take it that you don't know what it says?" asked Lucy.

"Billy and I both tried, but it's indecipherable," said Alice.

"You know, that guy who runs the school library, what's his name?" said Lucy.

"Mr Renaird?" said Alice.

"Yeah, that's it. We solved the case of the ghost haunting his library," said Lucy.

"Which turned out to be his own brother, trying to scare him away so he could take over the library," said Alice.

"Yeah, not a very nice guy. You remember the language he used when the police took him away?" said Lucy.

"I'm sure glad he didn't take over. His effect on the next generation of kids....I dread to think," said Alice.

"Anyway, Mr Renaird is also a researcher, often looking through various ancient books. And he even has a hobby of decoding," said Lucy.

"You mean like a mathematician?" asked Alice.

"No, not equations. Ancient letters and manuscripts that have been deemed indecipherable, he decodes them and rewrites as much as he can find on new paper," said Lucy.

"So, you think he can decipher the letter?" asked Alice.

"Seeing as it's the only lead we've got, I think it's worth trying," said Lucy.

"Alright then, we'll visit him in school tomorrow and see what he says," said Alice as she and Lucy felt good.

They had a very promising lead.

Billy then came into the room; he didn't look too happy.

"Billy, what happened out there? Is there any damage to the town?" asked Alice.

"Two houses were bombed; one fared slightly better, the other was completely demolished. There was a married couple in that one…..they didn't make it," said Billy.

"Oh, that's horrible," said Lucy.

"Yeah, yeah, it is," said Billy, as Alice noticed his expression change.

"I know that look; that's your thinking face; I remember it," said Alice.

"What is it?" asked Lucy.

"Well, while I was down there, I heard a couple of those Home Guard chaps talking, so I got close and eavesdropped a bit. They said this is the fifth air strike to hit the town during this month," said Billy.

"And each time, they've never seen the planes coming until they're just overhead of the town. Somehow, they aren't being picked up by the early warning devices along the coastline," said Billy.

"So, either they're getting better at keeping a low profile or…" Lucy didn't finish the last bit.

"Or there's a spy in town", so Alice did.

"But that can't be right. A spy, here? What could they want with Millstone?" asked Lucy.

"Same as everywhere else, probably. Bomb a couple of houses, kill a few dozen people, frighten everyone else into thinking that they're winning the war," said Billy.

"You don't think....if there is a spy....that he could have something to do with Tyler?" asked Lucy.

"I don't think we should rule it out," said Alice.

"Look, Alice, not that I'm trying to discourage you, but you said it yourself. Doctor Arthur has proven that Tyler's attack was attempted murder; the police won't think it was a bad robbery anymore. Why not just leave them to it?" said Billy.

"Even with the evidence, how long do you think it will take them to find the man? And after the air raid, they're going to have their hands full picking up the pieces," said Alice.

"Tyler is still in hospital, and if the attacker learns that, what's to stop him from trying again and maybe succeeding?" said Alice.

"Alice is right; it's up to us to solve this. We have to," said Lucy.

"Are you still with us, Billy?" asked Alice as Billy sighed.

"Of course I am; I just don't want either of you in any danger. Tyler would never forgive me," said Billy.

"That's why we have you, Billy. I think Tyler would feel better knowing that you're here to protect us," said Lucy.

"Yeah, I guess so," said Billy.

"Okay then, that's the plan. We will go to see Mr Reinard tomorrow and get this letter translated. With luck, it'll hold answers as to why this happened to Tyler," said Alice.

"And if it doesn't?" asked Lucy.

"Then we're back to square one," said Alice.

Chapter 10

Time for School

<u>Millstone on Sea, the next morning, 8:15 am</u>

The next day came as the residents of Millstone were still cleaning up the mess from the air raid. Each of the last five air raids had set fire to a high street or bombed a building or two. The Home Guards were puzzled as to how they couldn't see the planes coming until they were right over the town; the likelihood of there being a spy in town, helping the Nazi planes to avoid detection and telling them where to strike was becoming even more possible. But to this day, the spy hasn't been caught despite the Home Guard stepping up patrols of the town and the coastline.

Alice was allowed back into school; she couldn't be given too much compassionate leave. She always walked to school with Lucy, but Billy accompanied them this time.

"You didn't need to walk with us, Billy" said Alice.

"Ah, it's no problem; I am supposed to be the bodyguard after all. Plus, when your mother makes the request, I don't think it's wise to refuse her," said Billy.

"Okay, so once we're in school, we'll find Mr Reinard and ask him to help decipher the letter," said Lucy.

"That's the plan. Once we know its contents, we'll go from there," said Alice.

"You know, there's still every chance it could just be a love letter, one that Tyler meant to give to Veronica but wasn't able to," said Billy.

"Well, we'll find out, one way or another," said Alice.

Suddenly, someone called out Billy's name; everyone stopped and turned as two men in army uniform approached them. Billy recognised who they were straight away.

"Trevor, Coltan, what are you guys doing here?" asked Billy.

"We requested some leave ourselves. When we found out you were in Millstone, we came here to find you," said Trevor.

"There's something we need to talk about; something's happened," said Coltan.

"Did you hear about Tyler?" asked Alice.

"No, what about Tyler?" asked Trevor.

"Tyler's in hospital; someone tried to kill him two days ago," said Billy.

"No way, that's...that's unbelievable," said Trevor.

"You're Tyler's sister, aren't you?" asked Coltan.

"I am, I'm Alice. You guys know about me?" said Alice.

"Of course, Tyler talks forever about you in the camp. We're very sorry for what's happened; we hope he recovers soon," said Trevor.

"Me too," said Alice.

"Billy, we really need to talk to you, like now," said Coltan.

"Can you girls walk yourselves to school?" asked Billy.

"We've done it loads of times; we'll be fine," said Lucy.

"And we'll tell Mum that we felt very safe with you walking with us," said Alice.

Billy smiled and walked away with Trevor and Coltan. Alice and Lucy walked the rest of the way to school.

<u>Millstone on Sea School, Morning, 8:30 am</u>

The Millstone school welcomed students of all ages and promised a good education; any troublemakers were not tolerated, and the school generally had a good reputation. Alice and Lucy arrived and made their way inside the building, then headed for the library towards the back of the building. The library was quite small but still had a variety of books available. Mr Reinard was the head librarian and researcher; if anyone could decipher the letter, it would be him.

Alice and Lucy entered the library and found Mr Reinard sitting at his small desk. He looked up and smiled when he saw them.

"Lucy, Alice, what a pleasant surprise," said Mr Reinard.

"Hello, Mr Reinard," said Lucy.

"Can I help you both with something? Do you need to borrow a book?" asked Mr Reinard.

"Actually, we were hoping to make use of your…other skills, Mr Reinard," said Alice.

"Oh, I see. What can I do for you?" asked Mr Reinard.

"Lucy told me that you're good at deciphering old letters and manuscripts, no matter how much dirt and grime is on them. So I was hoping you could do the same for this," said Alice as she pulled out the letter and handed it to Mr Reinard.

"Oh my, this is quite a stain. What is this, wine, red ink? No, that's not possible; it's not been available for ages," said Mr Reinard.

"It's not wine, it's….it's.." Alice couldn't finish.

"It's Tyler's blood, Alice's brother", so Lucy did.

"Oh, oh my, I see. I heard about your brother, Alice; I'm very sorry for what you and your family are going through," said Mr Reinard.

"Thank you," said Alice.

"This is why we need your help, Mr Reinard. We're hoping that letter may contain answers, or at least half-answers as to why this happened to Tyler," said Lucy.

"Can you help us?" asked Alice.

"Normally, I'd have to put this at the bottom of the pile since I have a substantial workload ahead of me," said Mr Reinard.

"But, since you girls are the reason I'm not afraid to step inside my own library anymore, I'll try to get it finished by the end of the school day", said Mr Reinard.

"Thank you, Mr Reinard. We're very grateful," said Alice.

"Speaking of which, I think you two should be getting to class; it's about to start", said Mr Reinard, pointing at his pocket watch.

"Oh my, we're going to be late, come on, Lucy!" said Alice as they both ran out of the library and to their first class.

Miss Sewell was their English teacher, and she disliked tardiness. Alice and Lucy arrived in the classroom with only seconds to spare before the bell.

"We're very sorry we're late, Miss Sewell," said Alice.

"That's okay, Alice; according to the clock, you both had about four seconds to spare. So I won't mark you both down for tardiness," said Miss Sewell.

"Thank you, Miss Sewell," said Alice.

"Yes, thank you, miss, it won't happen again," said Lucy as she and Alice found their desks and sat down.

"Just make sure it doesn't. Now then, everyone, since we're all here, the class can begin," said Miss Sewell as she started her lecture of the day.

Alice and Lucy always did their best to pay attention; no good would come if they did poorly in class, even if the teacher was a bit boring at times.

Marigold Tea Room, Morning, 9:05 am

Billy took Trevor and Coltan to the Marigold tea room so they could tell him their news. A young waitress named Kate brought their coffee over.

"Here we are, gentlemen," said Kate.

"Thanks, darling," said Billy as he reached for some money, but Kate stopped him.

"First serving for soldiers is always the house," said Kate as she walked away.

"Nice one, cheers," said Trevor as everyone picked up their cups, clinked them and took a sip.

"Now then, what's this important news you guys have to tell me?" asked Billy.

Coltan and Trevor both looked at each other nervously before they answered.

"Patrick is dead," said Trevor.

"What?!" asked Billy, nearly choking on his drink.

"Patrick is dead, Billy; he was killed in action," said Coltan.

"What…but….Tyler and I didn't even leave that long ago; what happened?" said Billy.

"We were on a scouting run in the ruins of this city, trying to find confirmation of a Nazi presence and their military strength," said Trevor.

"We made our way from building to building, making sure it was clear before moving. But just when we were approaching the city centre, a sniper fired at us," said Coltan.

"Got Patrick right in the chest; he never had a chance," said Trevor.

"Oh my god…..did you recover his body?" said Billy.

"We did, thankfully. The sniper was pretty quick to retreat, so we managed to get Patrick out of there; he was being shipped home as we left," said Trevor.

"We're very sorry to tell you like this, Billy, especially after what happened to Tyler. How is he doing?" said Coltan.

"Not great. The doctors say he's stabilised but bleeding internally; if they can't fix it....he won't make it," said Billy.

"This would be a really bad time to mention your conspiracy theory, Coltan," said Trevor.

"Shut up, Trevor, it's not a theory. It is, but it's based on facts," said Coltan.

"Wait, what theory?" asked Billy.

"Coltan thinks we're cursed," said Trevor.

"I said shut up!" said Coltan.

"Okay, why do you think that?" asked Billy.

"Look, ever since we took the, you know what, a couple of months ago, I was getting this strange feeling," said Coltan.

"Here we go," said Trevor.

"It's a feeling of dread, and I've been having these nightmares. Things that have started to come true," said Coltan.

"In the last few weeks, Andy was killed by a grenade, a sniper shot Patrick, and now Tyler is in the hospital with internal bleeding. I'm not necessarily saying it's a curse, but it feels like something is coming after us all," said Coltan.

"You see what I've had to put up with; he hasn't shut up about this since you guys left," said Trevor.

"Well, what about the smuggler? Have you heard from him?" asked Billy.

"The last letter I got from him, which was shortly after Andy's death, said that the, you know what is secure in a safe place, but...." said Coltan.

"But what?" asked Billy.

"He's worried. The Nazis have been trying to track him down; they've nearly found his hideout a few times. He said if they get too close, he'll have to move the, you know what, to a backup location," said Coltan.

"Where?" asked Billy.

"He said he'll tell me in his next letter," said Coltan.

"Oh, this is getting too much. I still say we should take our bits of the, you know what," Billy interrupted Trevor.

"I made it clear to Tyler that if any of the squad tried to skirt around the pact, I'd go and confess everything to the Home Office," said Billy.

"You'd really snitch on us?" asked Trevor.

"Not important right now. What matters is that Alice, Lucy, and I are trying to find out who attacked Tyler. If we can find him, then maybe we can get some answers," said Billy.

"I'm sorry, did you say Alice and Lucy? Aren't those girls twelve years old?" asked Trevor with a slight laugh.

"They know what they're doing, trust me. And believe it or not, they may be the best chance of finding this bastard," said Billy.

"All we have to do is make sure that she doesn't find out about the, you know what. We need her 'cause if she finds out the truth, God help us," said Billy.

Miss Sewell's Class, Morning, 12:00 pm

The school bell rang for lunchtime, something that was a relief to many students who wanted to get out of the classroom and away from Miss Sewell.

"Alright, class, place your books on my desk when you leave so I can mark them. Miss Sherlock, can you stay a few minutes? I'd like a word with you," said Miss Sewell.

Alice gave an unsure look at Lucy as she and everyone else exited the classroom. Alice then walked to Miss Sewell's desk.

"Have I done something wrong, Miss?" asked Alice.

"Oh no, of course not. I didn't mean to give the impression you were in trouble; I just wanted a quick word," said Miss Sewell.

"I've read your recent book report, and it's very good. Your penmanship is neat and tidy, it's easy to understand, and you go into detail without it getting too boring," said Miss Sewell.

"Now, I know you are fascinated with Sherlock Holmes, but I wanted to ask. Have you considered reading…other books, Anne of Green Gables perhaps?" said Miss Sewell.

"To be honest, Miss, I have tried before. My mum suggested Anne of Green Gables. I've also tried Journey to the Centre of the Earth, The Wizard of Oz, and a number of other genres. But none of them have taken my interest like Mr Holmes," said Alice.

"I understand, Alice. When you develop a liking to a particular fictional character, who keeps getting adventures, it's tough to try anything different from it," said Miss Sewell.

"But I'm not saying it's bad, and your work shows it. Just try to consider it for the future," said Miss Sewell.

"I will, Miss," said Alice.

"Alright then, go and get your lunch," said Miss Sewell as Alice smiled, grabbed her coat and left the classroom.

Chapter 11

The Case of the Stolen Cash Box

School Yard/Miss Lorraine's Classroom, Afternoon, 12:30 pm

Alice met Lucy in the school cafeteria, and they ate lunch together. A while after, once they'd let the food go down a bit, they were both in the yard, playing with hoops, spinning them around their waists.

"I don't know why some girls have a problem with these hoop things. They're actually quite easy to use," said Lucy.

"Yeah, they also seem to stimulate the mind and help you focus," said Alice.

"I don't think I've reached that point yet, but I'll take your word for it," said Lucy.

"Miss Sherlock, Miss Porter," said a voice that came from a bespectacled woman in her thirties approaching them.

"Miss Lorraine," said Alice as she and Lucy stopped spinning their hoops.

Hilda Lorraine was of Spanish origin and one of the few foreign women who was allowed a teaching position in an English school. But she got on well with the students and had some respect from the other teachers, except the headmistress, who was still warming up to her.

"Sorry to disrupt your hooping, but I was hoping to have a talk with you both," said Miss Lorraine.

"Is something wrong?" asked Lucy.

"Kind of, yes. You see, I was hoping to make use of your....investigation skills," said Miss Lorraine.

"How can we help?" asked Alice.

"Not here, too many people listening. Let's go to my classroom," said Miss Lorraine as Alice and Lucy grabbed their coats and followed her inside.

Miss Lorraine led the girls into her classroom and shut the door.

"So, what's going on?" asked Lucy.

"Here's the thing. This morning, I collected the lunch money from my students, like I always do, and put it in my cashbox, which I then placed in the desk drawer and locked, " said Miss Lorraine.

"After the bell went and I dismissed my class, I went to get some lunch, then came back to prepare for the next lesson. But when I came in, something felt....off, um, wrong," said Miss Lorraine.

"What was wrong?" asked Alice.

"Just a feeling that something was out of place. That was when I noticed the drawer (she pulled the drawer open and showed the scratches around the keyhole). It'd been jimmied open," said Miss Lorraine.

"And when I looked inside, my cash box was gone," said Miss Lorraine.

"You think someone stole it?" asked Alice.

"It's the only explanation I can come up with. But the problem with that is I always lock the door when I go out, and I always keep the key with me," said Miss Lorraine.

"So, whoever took your cash box didn't just get past a locked drawer, but a locked door too," said Lucy.

"That's why I've asked you both here. I really need your help to make sense of this and get my cash box back," said Miss Lorraine.

"Miss Lorraine, obviously we're more than happy to help you, but isn't something like this best reported to the headmistress?" said Alice.

"Let me explain something, Alice. The headmistress has disliked my presence ever since I first arrived here. She believes that a foreigner working in an English school…taints the atmosphere," said Miss Lorraine.

"She said that to you?" asked Lucy.

"No, I heard her talking to Mr Clive in the corridor one time. He tried to defend me, bless him," said Miss Lorraine.

"But suffice it to say that if the headmistress learns that I not only let someone break into my classroom but also steal my cash box, it's just the excuse she needs to fire me," said Miss Lorraine.

"Please, girls, I really need your help," said Miss Lorraine.

"Okay, Miss Lorraine, we'll take the case," said Alice as Miss Lorraine smiled with relief.

"So where do we start?" asked Lucy.

"Let's start by figuring out just how easy it is to get past this door without a key," said Alice as she stepped outside the classroom.

"Miss Lorraine, can you lock the door please?" asked Alice as Miss Lorraine closed the door and locked it.

Alice began to check just how sturdy the door was. It seemed like it could withstand an attempt to force entry, and when Alice used one of her spare hair pins to try and lockpick the door, it didn't get very far.

"Okay, could you let me back in, please?" asked Alice as Miss Lorraine unlocked the door.

"Well, from the outside, there's no sign that someone kicked the door in, especially if it was still locked when you got back, and trying with a hairpin didn't seem to work either," said Alice.

"So whoever broke in must have had the key," said Lucy.

"But that's impossible. I told you, I keep the key on me at all times; it's never out of my sight," said Miss Lorraine.

"What bothers me is that if, and it's only an if, Miss Lorraine, the thief had the key to the class and the drawer, why would he need to force it open?" said Alice.

"Ah, I think I can explain that bit. Mr Clive once told me that the desk I have is a "problem desk". Apparently, the key only turns so far; the last tumbler won't cooperate, I think he said, so you have to tug to fully open it", said Miss Lorraine.

"So the thief may have tried to get in with the key, but when it wouldn't work, he then decided to jimmy the drawer open," said Lucy.

"Miss Lorraine, can you think of anyone who'd do this to you?" asked Alice.

"Not off the top of my head, no. All the other teachers have been nice to me, and the students seem to like me; I can't think why any of them would do something like this," said Miss Lorraine.

"What about the headmistress? You did say she's looking for any excuse to fire you," said Alice.

"Yeah, but it's the headmistress Alice. She may be a strict woman with a temper, but is she really someone who'd frame a teacher for theft just to fire them?" said Lucy.

"Well, this is tricky, but I don't think we'll have much time to investigate more. Look at the clock; it's nearly time for the next class," said Alice.

"But it's okay, girls. I checked the register, and you two are with me next," said Miss Lorraine.

"Well, yeah, but I don't see how we can just waltz out of class to go looking for clues," said Lucy.

"If you both ask to use the bathroom, then you'll have a reason to leave the class. After that, it's up to you where you go next," said Miss Lorraine.

"Our first time leaving class to go sneak around the school looking for a missing cash box. What does Mr Holmes say, "Sometimes things happen for a reason", right?" said Lucy.

"Sometimes he does, but he also says the game is afoot," said Alice.

Miss Lorraine's Class, Afternoon, 1:05 pm

Five minutes after the class came in and took their seats, and Miss Lorraine handed out the day's assignment, Alice checked the clock and signalled to Lucy that it was time to make their move.

"Miss Lorraine," said Alice, raising her hand.

"Yes, Miss Sherlock?" said Miss Lorraine.

"Lucy and I need to use the bathroom," said Alice.

"Of course, on you go, girls," said Miss Lorraine as Alice and Lucy casually got up from their seats and left the classroom.

Once outside, they started tiptoeing down the corridor and away from the room.

"Okay, what do we do now?" asked Lucy.

"Well, I know Miss Lorraine said she didn't know anyone who'd do this to her. But I think she was lying," said Alice.

"How could you tell?" asked Lucy.

"Her glasses," said Alice.

"Her glasses?" asked Lucy.

"You remember that game she played with us three weeks ago when she gave us facts, and we had to figure out if she was telling the truth or lying? When she told us one that was a lie, she always adjusted her glasses," said Alice.

"Oh, and when you asked if she knew anyone who'd steal from her, she did it then," said Lucy.

"Exactly, and the way I see it, there's only one place where we can figure out who'd have it in for her," said Alice.

"Oh no, Alice, please don't say it," said Lucy.

"We're going to the headmistress's office," said Alice as she walked away.

"And you said it," said Lucy as she followed.

The girls crept down the corridors and headed toward the headmistress's office, but Lucy wasn't sure about it.

"Are we seriously about to break into the office of the scariest woman in the school?!" asked Lucy.

"It's not really breaking in; she never locks her door anyway. She thinks because everyone is so scared of her that they wouldn't dare to enter her office when she isn't there," said Alice.

"And she'd be right; I'm one of them!" said Lucy as they arrived at the office door.

Alice peeped inside. It wasn't very clear glass, but you could always tell if someone was in by the large smudge that would walk back and forth.

"She's not there," said Alice.

"Alice, I'm begging you to think this through. If we get caught in there, we won't be given detention; we'll be expelled!" said Lucy.

"Listen, I just want to look in the folder where she keeps the complaints filed by teachers. I'll only be a moment, so keep an eye out," said Alice as she carefully entered the office.

Lucy stood guard, still bemused as to what Alice was doing.

Alice quietly closed the door and made her way over to the desk; it was in the centre of the room, which wasn't very big. She'd actually been called in once before after getting into a fight with another girl, all because she'd mocked Tyler's chances of living up to the real soldiers.

Alice opened the top desk drawer and pulled out the folder of complaints; she quickly and quietly looked through it. Lucy was pacing outside, checking the corridors for signs of the headmistress or anyone else coming. Alice then smiled as she found what she was looking for; she then put the folder back in the drawer and closed it.

Lucy then noticed the headmistress approaching down the right side corridor; she knocked on the door to the office.

"Hurry up, Alice, she's coming," said Lucy quietly.

Alice went for the door, but something caused her to stop in her tracks; she looked back and found part of her sleeve was caught in the drawer. Panic filled her as she tried to open the drawer to free herself, but now it was stuck. Lucy could see the headmistress getting closer, but there was no sign of Alice leaving the office. As Alice desperately tried to free herself, Lucy took the initiative and stepped out in front of the headmistress.

"Headmistress," said Lucy.

"Miss Porter, why aren't you in class?" asked the headmistress.

"Bathroom break," said Lucy.

"Then why are you wandering the halls?" asked the headmistress.

"I'm a little lost," said Lucy.

"How can you lose your way in school?" asked the headmistress.

As Lucy was thinking about how to answer, she saw Alice leave the office in the corner of her eye.

"I...just remembered the way back, temporary memory blank; sorry to bother you, headmistress," said Lucy as she tried to quickly run away.

"Miss Porter," said the headmistress as Lucy stopped; she feared she was busted.

"Don't run in the corridors", said the headmistress.

"Yes, of course, sorry, headmistress," said Lucy as she walked away.

The headmistress just shook her head and entered her office. Alice and Lucy were hiding around the corner of the left-side corridor. They both looked at each other and quietly started laughing.

"I can't believe we just did that," said Lucy.

"Me neither; my sleeve got caught, and I thought that was it," said Alice.

"You think that's bad? She's probably going to recommend me for a medical evaluation on account of my memory blanks," said Lucy.

"Oh, please tell me you found something," said Lucy.

"I always do. Out of all the reports in the file, only one was written by Miss Lorraine, and guess what? It was for Colin Seamus," said Alice.

"Mr Seamus, the janitor with the Irish accent?" asked Lucy.

"Yeah, apparently, Miss Lorraine filed a complaint that stated he tried to assault her while under the influence of alcohol sexually," said Alice.

"Oh my, you don't hear about things like that in school," said Lucy.

"Come on, I know where his closet is," said Alice as she and Lucy went to find Mr Seamus.

Colin Seamus was from Ireland and came over to find work nearly fourteen years ago. He settled for the janitor position in the school, which was not the most glamorous job, but at least it paid. Alice and Lucy arrived outside the closet door and knocked. Seamus came out; he was forty-three with grey hair.

"Hello, girls, can I help you?" said Seamus.

"We'd like to talk with you, Mr Seamus," said Alice.

"Don't call me mister, please; it makes me sound old. I'm only forty-three, and some of the cheeky girls around her keep calling me granddad," said Seamus.

"Now what's happening? Don't tell me they've sicked up in the cafeteria again. I've told them many times that those fish fingers are out of date," said Seamus.

"It's not the fish fingers. We'd like to talk to you about Miss Lorraine," said Lucy.

"Hilda, why, what's she said about me now?" asked Seamus.

"What we want to discuss will be almost as simple as cash in the box," said Alice as Seamus realised what they were referring to.

"We can talk here, or we can go and see the headmistress," said Lucy.

"Maybe you should both come inside; I'll tell you everything, promise", said Seamus as Alice and Lucy walked inside the closet; there was enough room for everyone.

"Okay then, how much do you both know?" asked Seamus.

"We know a little, but the rest will come when you answer one question for us. Did you take Miss Lorraine's cash box?" said Alice.

"Aye, I did," said Seamus.

"Why?" asked Lucy.

"Because I wanted to get back at her for costing me my job, the only one I've had since coming to this county fourteen years ago!" said Seamus.

"You mean because of the complaint she filed against you?" asked Alice.

"Aye, not one of my best moments. I....I admit....I may have had a slight crush on Hilda when she came here three years ago, but I knew nothing could happen. She's young and attractive, and what about me? Not even sixty and already with grey hair," said Seamus.

"During the nights, when I've finished my shifts, I like to have a little drink. Sometimes I go to the pub, and sometimes I keep a bottle in the closet," said Seamus.

"But that particular night...I may have been fantasising about me and Hilda, so I drank a bit more than I usually did. I didn't even remember going into her class while she was there, let alone what she said about me trying to unbutton her shirt," said Seamus.

"When I woke up the next morning, it all came back to me like a thunderbolt. I couldn't rush out because of the hangover, but when I was ready, I dashed to the school to apologise. And what did I find? She'd already gone behind my back and tattled on me to the headmistress," said Seamus.

"She served me my week's notice on the spot (he went over to the shelf, removed a sponge that was hiding the cash box and picked it up). So I wanted to get back at Hilda for taking everything away from me," said Seamus.

"By getting her fired?" asked Lucy.

"I wanted her to know what it was like to be chewed out and not given the chance to explain things and apologise. I know what I did was wrong, but what she did was worse," said Seamus.

"Here, you best give it back to her. And while she probably won't accept it, tell her I'm very sorry," said Seamus as he tried to hand the cash box to Alice.

"Actually, Seamus, I think we have a better idea," said Alice.

"We do?" asked Lucy.

Alice took a moment to explain her plan to Seamus before she and Lucy returned to Miss Lorraine's class.

"There you both are; I was getting worried," said Miss Lorraine.

"Sorry, miss, personal matter," said Lucy.

"Well, back to your desks and get on with your work, please," said Miss Lorraine as Lucy returned to her seat, but Alice went to Miss Lorraine.

"I have a message from the headmistress," said Alice.

"Oh dear, what is it?" said Miss Lorraine as Alice whispered something in her ear.

"Ah, okay. Thank you, Miss Sherlock," said Miss Lorraine as Alice went back to her seat, and she and Lucy started with their assignment.

Miss Lorraine's Classroom, Afternoon, 3:30 pm

Alice and Lucy surprisingly managed to finish the assignment before the bell for the end of the day went; they were quite good at keeping up with school work despite losing time. As Miss Lorraine dismissed the class, Alice and Lucy remained behind with her.

"So, you said I'd be getting my cash box back?" asked Miss Lorraine.

"You will; in fact, it should be coming right about (Seamus entered the class) now", said Alice.

"Miss Lorraine," said Seamus.

"Colin, um, Mr Seamus, what are you doing here?" asked Miss Lorraine.

"I'm here to return something to you," said Seamus, placing the cash box on the desk.

"My cash box, you took it?" asked Miss Lorraine.

"I tried to do a terrible thing to you that unfortunate night, Hilda, and I can't even begin to tell you how truly sorry I am", said Seamus.

"But I didn't appreciate that you never even gave me the chance to say it; you just went behind my back to the headmistress and got me fired. Fourteen years down the drain because of you," said Seamus.

"So I wanted to get back at you the only way I knew how, making you feel what it was like to have your one and only job robbed from underneath you", said Seamus.

"But I allowed my judgement to cloud my feelings; alcohol is something that I should've kicked years ago. I shouldn't have stooped to such an underhanded trick; I'm sorry," said Seamus.

"Now, if you don't mind, I need to finish my shift before packing up the last of my stuff," said Seamus as he started to walk away.

"Colin, wait," said Miss Lorraine as Seamus stopped and turned around.

"I, too, know the vices of alcohol. My parents supported prohibition in the 1930s, but....I didn't; I know what it can do to your mind," said Miss Lorraine.

"You are right; I should've given you the chance to explain things, even apologise. But I was so shaken up as it was the first time it's happened, I didn't think about you. I thought I was doing the right thing; I'm very sorry, Colin," said Miss Lorraine.

"Listen, why don't we both go and see the headmistress, see if we can withdraw my complaint and get you your job back?" said Miss Lorraine.

"Trying to convince the strictest woman in school to go back on a decision where she always has the final say? I like a challenge," said Colin, and he and Miss Lorraine smiled.

"Alice, Lucy, I can't thank you both enough for this. You've saved my job and given me the chance to save someone else's," said Miss Lorraine.

"It's our pleasure, Miss Lorraine," said Alice as everyone exited the classroom.

Miss Lorraine and Seamus went to the headmistress's office, and Alice and Lucy headed back to the library.

They arrived just in time as Mr Reinard was getting his coat on.

"Mr Reinard," said Lucy.

"Ah, there you girls are. I was worried you'd forgotten about me and gone home," said Mr Reinard.

"How did it go with the letter?" asked Alice.

"It was quite the challenge. Dirt and grime is one thing, but dried blood is more difficult than it looks," said Mr Reinard.

"Sorry," said Alice.

"No, don't be sorry; I appreciated the chance to hone my skills. Anyway, I just finished the last sentence, speaking of which, there's only four written," said Mr Reinard.

"Only four sentences? What do they say?" asked Lucy.

Mr Reinard read the letter.

"The dreaded Eagles are on the march.

The treasure will have to be moved.

It's been placed for safety in the Dragon's Cave.

And is protected by a Guardian of such disdain."

Alice and Lucy looked at each other.

"What?!" they both said.

"That's what I thought," said Mr Reinard as he handed the letter to Alice.

"But...this doesn't make any sense. Is this really all that was written?" said Alice.

"Just that I'm afraid there's nothing else in the letter," said Mr Reinard.

"Alice, I'm sorry, but I don't think that letter is going to help at all," said Lucy.

"It has to. Tyler wouldn't have had it on him if it had just been a scrap of paper. It has to mean something," said Alice.

"Well, it sounds to me like a riddle, but it's just not written in very good English. What we need is a translator, but who can we ask for help?" said Lucy as Alice thought for a moment.

"There is one person who can help," said Alice.

Chapter 12

A Crushing Secret

Millstone on Sea Park, Afternoon, 3:55 pm.

Alice and Lucy went to the park to find Billy; Alice remembered that he liked to go there when it was empty for a smoke. He was just finishing a cigarette when they saw him sitting on one of the park benches.

"Hey, girls. Oh blimey, was I supposed to pick you both up from school?" said Billy.

"No, it's okay, Billy. But we would like to talk with you," said Lucy.

"Okay, so long as it's not "What's the meaning of the universe?" then we're good," said Billy as Alice showed him the letter, and his expression dropped.

"You know what this means, don't you, Billy?" asked Alice.

"Got no idea," said Billy.

"Don't….don't play games with us, Billy. You've been acting strangely ever since we found this letter. Like at every opportunity, you've tried to dissuade us from looking into it," said Alice.

"And when we found it in the alley, and you tried to read it, you went all quiet. Because you were starting to realise what it said, and you kept it from us," said Alice.

"What does it mean? Why did Tyler have it? What have you been up to?!" asked Alice.

Billy sighed as he let out the smoke he'd just inhaled. He knew that there was no chance of making something up to get out of this; Alice and Lucy were too smart for him.

"Sit down, both of you; I'll try to tell you everything," said Billy.

"Just remember one thing: Billy, Lucy, and I are very good at figuring out whether someone is lying to us," said Alice.

"I won't lie to you, I promise. Just sit down first," said Billy as Alice and Lucy sat next to him on the bench.

"For the record, Tyler wanted you kept out of this, Alice. He didn't want you to be in any sort of danger," said Billy.

"What did Tyler want to keep me out of?" asked Alice.

"We...did something a couple of months ago, and it's weighed heavily on each of our consciences ever since," said Billy.

"There was this farm the Nazis had taken. They'd slaughtered the family who lived there and set up a communications post. The mission was simple:

eradicate the Germans and destroy the radio," said Billy.

"We laid low for a bit, made our plans and came up with a strategy. We took the farm with no real trouble, but something puzzled us. There were nearly forty Nazis alone guarding that place; with one radio, it seemed a bit much," said Billy.

"Afterwards, we searched the farmhouse, making sure no one was hiding in the dark so they could stick a knife in our backs. Tyler and I checked the basement; it was mostly open, so we could see what was in there," said Billy.

"But something stood out, a single door that seemed to lead to another room. We both had the same feeling. "Why was it there?" we both thought," Billy said.

"We tried to open the door, but we found it wasn't easy since it was heavily secured. Metal bolts and chains, the works. So we found some of the explosives the Nazis had and blew the door open," said Billy.

"We got the rest of the squad and checked inside. And what we found….we couldn't believe our eyes," said Billy.

"What did you find?" asked Lucy.

"Gold, lots and lots of gold bars," said Billy.

"Gold? What was it doing on a farm?" asked Alice.

"Well, there had been some rumours going around the camps. Apparently, spies in Berlin had told British Intelligence that Hitler was shipping stacks from his gold reserve to hide in other countries. In case Berlin should fall, so long as Hitler escaped, he wouldn't have lost everything," said Billy.

"How much was in there?" asked Lucy.

"We tried to count it, but as it seemed to keep going on, we gave up. But by the time we'd stopped, our estimate was at nearly two hundred," said Billy.

"Two hundred?!" asked Alice.

"Yeah, we felt that maybe it was fate or just pure luck that it happened to us," said Billy.

"But, what did you do with the gold?" asked Lucy.

"Well, we had to think about that. What do we do, tell the Home Office, fill our pockets? No, none of those. So we came up with hiding it somewhere safe," said Billy.

"How did you move it?" asked Lucy.

"Coltan put us in touch with a smuggler. Bloke was well known around the camps and capable of getting almost unreachable things. We told him of our predicament, and he agreed to take the gold to his hideout and keep it safe for us," said Billy.

"Wait, the letter that Andy wrote to Wesley, the one that talked about a pact. That was true, wasn't it?" asked Alice.

"Yes, Alice, it was. The pact was a form of protection we came up with, something to stop us from killing each other over the gold," said Billy.

"So, what did you plan to do with the gold?" asked Lucy.

"The pact stated that the gold would remain in hiding until after the war. Then, so long as any of us were still alive, we'd take our shares and use them to support our families and maybe splash out a bit on some luxuries," said Billy.

Alice got up and walked a few steps forward; she was deep in thought about what she'd just heard.

"Alice, I'm really sorry you had to hear it like this. Like I said, Tyler wanted you kept out of it; he didn't want you to have the burden of keeping it a secret," said Billy.

Alice turned around to look at Billy.

"I just have one more question, Billy, and I want you to think very carefully before you answer," said Alice.

"Okay," said Billy.

"Whose idea was it to take the gold?" asked Alice.

Billy was quiet.

"Whose idea was it, Billy?!" Alice asked again.

"(sigh) It was Tyler's," said Billy.

Alice was now shocked even more than she already was. Lucy got up and went over to her.

"Alice, I know that this has all come as a shock- A shock?!" Alice interrupted Lucy.

"Lucy, I can't even begin to comprehend how much of a shock this has been to me. How could he do this?!" said Alice with tears in her eyes.

"So, as it turns out, I never really knew my brother after all," said Alice as she walked away.

"Don't say that, Alice, Alice!" said Lucy as she called after her, but Alice didn't respond and just kept walking.

Lucy and Billy remained behind, thinking about what had just transpired and how much Alice's heart had been broken.

Beachfront outside Sherlock Household, Afternoon, 4:45 pm

After walking around town for a bit, Alice found her way down to the beach in front of her house. She'd removed her socks and shoes and had a paddle in the sea. Standing there and letting the breeze blow through her hair is what she did when she wanted peace or time to think, and she had a lot to think about.

"How is the investigation going?" suddenly said Sherlock Holmes, who'd reappeared next to Alice.

"I was beginning to wonder where you'd gone, Mr Holmes," said Alice.

"I figured that it was appropriate to only appear when you needed me. If you need help, advice or encouragement, and something tells me you could use it," said Sherlock.

"Can I ask you something, Mr Holmes? Is it wrong to want to quit on a case?" asked Alice.

"There are no quitters, Alice, only those who give up. And from what I've seen, that's not who you are," said Sherlock.

"When I first started this case, it was because I wanted to help my brother, to find out who attacked him. And now it seems that he may have been the reason behind it," said Alice.

"I don't think he intended to get stabbed, Alice," said Sherlock.

"That's not the point, Mr Holmes. He and his friends stole a ton of gold from the Germans; they had to know it would come back on them," said Alice.

"When untold riches and wealth suddenly surround a person, and they have the choice to take the money or go back to living destitute, you can always see which choice is the one picked", said Sherlock.

"I just can't believe that he would do that; that's not the Tyler I know," said Alice.

"To this day, people still don't understand that becoming rich, either from earning or stealing, always comes with a price. Most believe they need it to be happy and alive, but all it does is make them greedy and selfish and, in most cases, gives them a compulsion to kill," said Sherlock.

"I don't think you really want to give up the case, Alice. I think that you're still trying to process this secret you've found out and how it's going to affect your relationship with your brother," said Sherlock.

"Maybe. But Billy says that none of them knows where the gold is, and we're still no closer to finding who tried to kill Tyler," said Alice.

"Perhaps instead of focusing on the gold and where it is, try to think about the suspects who are closer to home," said Sherlock.

"You mean the rest of the squad?" asked Alice.

"Billy may claim that this pact is supposed to protect them from each other. But how does it really stop one or more of them from wanting a bigger share?" said Sherlock.

"Look into them, Alice. Find out where their loyalties really lie. In comradeship, or filthy riches," said Sherlock.

"Alice!" suddenly said Lucy as she was walking down the beach towards her. Alice looked back and saw Sherlock Holmes was gone again.

Lucy had also removed her socks and shoes as she came up to Alice.

"I thought I'd find you here," said Lucy.

"Yeah, I just needed to be alone to think a little for a while," said Alice.

"Well, I don't blame you; it's a nice view," said Lucy.

"Lucy, I'm really sorry for snapping at you earlier; I didn't mean to," said Alice.

"It's okay, Alice. For what it's worth, if it had been my brother who'd done something like that, I would've felt like I'd been kicked in the teeth, too," said Lucy.

"I'm just struggling to make sense of it all. Tyler spent years teaching me the difference between right and wrong when I was growing up. Then he suddenly steals a pile of gold?" said Alice.

"It wasn't just him that took it, though," said Lucy.

"I know, but it was still his idea. And it makes me wonder if his teachings meant anything," said Alice.

"You heard what Billy said; he was going to use his share to support his family; they all were, buying luxuries was secondary. Tyler is a good man with a good heart, and you're always in his thoughts," said Lucy, and Alice smiled a little.

"Okay, let's revisit this another time. We still have a case to solve," said Alice, and Lucy smiled.

"Alright then, so where are we at the moment?" asked Lucy.

"The letter is a bust, but I've been thinking. How certain is Billy that this pact is supposed to protect the squad from each other?" said Alice.

"Yeah, a pact is really a promise; it's not a court order," said Lucy.

"Which doesn't stop any of them from wanting to take a bigger share," said Alice.

"Well, we know two are dead, and one is in the hospital," said Lucy.

"Wait, who's the second dead one?" asked Alice.

"Oh, sorry, Alice. Billy told me that after you left, he heard that another of the squad, a guy called Patrick, was killed in action," said Lucy.

"Oh gosh, so who does that leave us with?" asked Alice.

"Three by my count, Coltan, Trevor and Billy," said Lucy.

"Not Billy; he'd never hurt Tyler; I'd stake my life on it," said Alice.

"Me too. So that just leaves Trevor and Coltan," said Lucy.

"Hey, you cheered up a bit?" asked Lucy.

"A little, but not a lot," said Alice.

"You just need a reason to smile again and maybe laugh too. My Mum says it's good for you," said Lucy.

"Yeah, come on, let's get back to the house," said Alice as they started to leave.

But Lucy turned too quickly as she suddenly stumbled and started to fall; Alice reached out and grabbed her but lost her balance, and they both fell down with a splash. They both looked at each other, and how wet they were, then they started laughing.

"I told you you'd find a reason to laugh," said Lucy.

"You did that on purpose," said Alice as they picked themselves up.

"No, I didn't," said Lucy.

"Yes, you did!" said Alice as she splashed Lucy.

"No, I didn't!" said Lucy as she splashed Alice.

Soon, the two of them were splashing about and laughing their heads off, and for a moment, they completely forgot about what had transpired in the last few hours.

Sherlock Household, Afternoon, 5:10 pm

After they'd tired themselves out, Alice and Lucy both went back to the house. Mavis wasn't too happy about how soaking wet they were, but she was just glad to see Alice smiling. Jasper gave both of the girls a bathrobe to change into while he took their wet clothes to dry on the washing line. Lucy was waiting in Alice's room when she came in with a towel for both their wet hair.

"Here you are," said Alice as she handed one to Lucy.

"Thanks," said Lucy.

"Okay, Jasper says that our clothes should be dry within the hour," said Alice.

"That quick?" asked Lucy.

"One of the perks of living by the cliffs is that the sea breeze does wonders with drying laundry quickly," said Alice.

"Thanks, Lucy; I don't care if that was on purpose or not; it was really fun," said Alice.

"No problem," said Lucy.

"So, when can we expect to see Billy?" asked Lucy.

"Well, Mum said she'll look for him while out shopping. I guess all we can do is wait," said Alice, and a knock at the door revealed Jasper.

"Miss Alice, Master Billy is here to see you," said Jasper.

"Thank you, Jasper; please show him in," said Alice.

"Right away, you can go in", said Jasper as he walked away, and Billy came into the room.

"Hey girls, whoa. Sorry, I didn't realise I was interrupting spa day," said Billy.

"You're not, Billy, it's…a long story," said Alice.

"Listen, Alice; I want you to know that I'm sorry for how you found things out. Tyler was only keeping it quiet because he didn't want you in danger or to have the burden of keeping it a secret," said Billy.

"When he took the gold, all he was thinking about was you and making sure that you had a future when the war ends….if the war ends", said Billy.

"Well, thank you for telling me, Billy; I know it can't have been easy," said Alice.

"So, are we good?" asked Billy as Alice hugged him.

"We're good," said Alice as she stopped hugging him.

"We're good too," said Lucy as she hugged Billy.

"If you're in love with me because I'm so handsome, you only have to say, Lucy," said Billy as Lucy laughed and stopped hugging him.

"So, where are we on the investigation?" asked Billy.

"Well, we do have another possible lead, but you might not like it too much," said Alice.

"Cor blimey, if it's any worse than recent events, then probably you're right," said Billy.

"How much do you know about Coltan and Trevor?" asked Lucy.

"Not a lot, really; I never even knew them until I signed up after the start of the war. We were in the same barracks and got on pretty well. It's why they made us a squad; they saw how well we all worked together, especially when Patrick and Andy came along," said Billy.

"That reminds me, Billy, I'm really sorry about Patrick," said Alice.

"Thank you, yeah, it was…a real shock," said Billy.

"There's that look on your face again," said Alice.

"Is it that easy to see?" asked Billy.

"Kind of, yeah. So what are you thinking?" said Alice.

"Just about how Patrick died; he was killed after being shot in the chest by a sniper. But I've seen him dodge bullets that were inches away from his face; he even managed to duck just before a sniper fired at him one time. So the fact he was taken by surprise, a lucky shot, no, something is wrong there," said Billy.

"You think he was murdered?" asked Lucy.

"I don't know, maybe. So anyway, you're both setting your sights on Trevor and Coltan now?" said Billy.

"Their sudden arrival only two days after Tyler was stabbed seemed a bit convenient, and with the gold on the line, they may be trying to circumvent the pact," said Alice.

"But only the smuggler knows where the gold is," said Billy.

"Who told you that, Coltan or Trevor?" asked Lucy.

"Well, Coltan did, he's friends with the....oh, I see. How do we know that he was telling the truth?" said Billy.

"We need to look into both of them before they leave town. Did they say where they were staying?" said Alice.

"Yeah, they both got a room at the George and Dragon; they have to share apparently," said Billy.

"There might be something there that connects them to Tyler, Patrick or something," said Alice.

"But Alice, we're in school tomorrow. I don't think our teacher will be too happy to let us out of class to go break into a room at the pub," said Lucy.

"You won't have to, I'll do it," said Billy.

"Are you sure, Billy? These are your brothers in arms," said Alice.

"I should've tried harder to stop the squad from taking the gold; maybe none of this would've happened. Besides, you two have been pouring your hearts and souls into this case; it's about time I do my bit," said Billy.

"We're grateful, Billy. Hopefully, this will turn up some answers we can use," said Alice.

"Well, all we can do now is wait for our clothes to dry, then I think I need to head back home", said Lucy as the sudden sound of the air raid siren rang out.

"Or, sleepover?" asked Alice.

"That works, too," said Lucy.

Alice retrieved her slippers from under the bed and put them on; she also had a spare pair for Lucy. Billy then led them out, and they joined Jasper and headed down into the shelter. Jack and Mavis were already there, along with a surprise visitor, Veronica.

"Are you both okay?" asked Jack.

"We're okay, Dad, are you and Mum?" said Alice.

"We're fine. Thanks to your mum, I have just returned from a shopping trip. I ran into Veronica, as you can see and brought her back with us. It seems she was already on her way here," said Jack.

Veronica looked as though she'd been crying. Mavis was trying to comfort her when Alice came over.

"What's wrong, Veronica?" asked Alice.

"It's…it's Tyler….they….they said his condition has worsened," said Veronica as she started crying again.

Everyone in the shelter had a new worry besides the German bombers.

Chapter 13

Gathering Proof

<u>George and Dragon Pub, the next morning, 9:05 am.</u>

While waiting in the shelter for the all-clear, Veronica further explained that the doctors had found the source of Tyler's internal bleeding, but the result was worse than they were expecting. They made a quick decision that Tyler needed to be taken in for a more in-depth surgery to fix him and stop the bleeding, but there was the chance that he might not make it, given that only a few survived the operation. Veronica had gone to visit Tyler when they told her, and she quickly tried making her way to tell the Sherlocks but slightly lost her way, given she was walking with tears in her eyes.

The air raid passed, and everyone chose to stay the night in the house. Mavis talked with Veronica to take their minds off things, and Alice and Lucy enjoyed their sleepover, mostly filled with talking about their favourite fictional detective. Billy stayed, but his mind was on other things. Could Coltan and, or Trevor, be responsible for Tyler's attack, for Patrick being killed? Had they even somehow contributed to Andy's death? The thoughts were there, and they weren't leaving. But Billy kept his word, and after dropping Alice and Lucy off at school, he headed for the George and Dragon pub and managed to persuade Tim to let him into the room.

Tim walked Billy upstairs to the room Coltan and Trevor were sharing.

"I can't believe I let you convince me to do this," said Tim.

"I really appreciate it, Tim; it's for a good cause," said Billy.

"If Mr Prosser finds out I let you into someone's room without permission, I'll get the sack," said Tim.

"Don't worry about it. If anything goes wrong, I'll just tell Mr Prosser it was all your idea," said Billy as Tim gave an unimpressed look.

"Kidding, now come on and open up", said Billy as Tim used his key to open the door.

"Alright, I'll just be a couple of minutes," said Billy as he entered the room. Tim stopped him and held out his hand.

"Fine," said Billy as he handed Tim a pound note.

"There's another for you if you can stand here and keep an eye out. Let me know if Coltan or Trevor are coming back," said Billy.

"Fine, just be quick," said Tim as Billy stepped into the room.

The room wasn't that big, with a single bed and wardrobe. But Billy could see that Trevor and Coltan had already made themselves comfortable; at least one of them was sleeping on the floor. He started looking through the wardrobe, and then, all around the bed, he found something hidden in the mattress. Billy pulled out a letter, read it and found it was addressed to Trevor and signed "Michelle".

"Trevor does have a girlfriend, but I thought her name was Rebecca," Billy said quietly.

He pocketed the letter and went back to searching the room.

Billy then started to search the kit bags. He found nothing of interest in Trevor's, but he did find something in Coltan's. It was a bottle of pills that he immediately recognised and gave a big sigh.

"Oh damn it, Coltan, you promised you'd stopped taking these," said Billy quietly to himself again.

He also pocketed the bottle and put the kit bags back together.

Once he was certain he'd found what he could, Billy made sure the room was exactly as he found it and quietly left. Tim was waiting and holding out his hand as Billy gave him the second-pound note he had promised. He then left the pub and headed for a new destination.

Nesbit (Old Boy) House, Morning, 9:15 am

Billy walked to the house of someone he hoped could help with what he'd discovered about Coltan; he arrived outside and knocked on the door. A woman in her sixties answered moments later.

"Oh, hello, Billy," said Mrs Nesbit.

"Hello, Mrs Nesbit, how are you?" said Billy.

"I'm well, thank you, and for goodness sake, call me Martha; I've told you often enough," said Mrs Nesbit.

"Forgive me, Martha," said Billy.

"So how can I help you?" asked Mrs Nesbit.

"I need to speak with your husband. Has he already gone to work?" said Billy.

"No, he's in the living room. He's been given the morning off; his work is trying out some new younger recruits," said Mrs Nesbit, whispering the last part.

"Oh, I see. So he's not in a good mood?" said Billy.

"Provided you don't bring it up, he's been perfect as pie. Come on in," said Mrs Nesbit as she invited Billy inside.

"Cup of tea?" asked Mrs Nesbit.

"No, thank you, Martha, I'm not staying long," said Billy.

"Chocolate biscuit?" said Mrs Nesbit.

"Never let it be said that Billy Desmond said no to a chocolate biscuit," said Billy.

"Alright, dearie, you go and have your talk with Andrew; I'll bring in the biscuits," said Mrs Nesbit.

"You're the best, Martha," said Billy as he went into the living room while Mrs Nesbit went to the kitchen.

Old Boy was sitting in an armchair with a newspaper.

"Ah, Billy, I thought that sounded like your voice," said Old Boy.

"Not deaf and blind yet, are you, Old Boy?" said Billy.

"Not a chance in hell; come and take a seat, son," said Old Boy as Billy sat in the armchair opposite him.

"So, to what do I owe the pleasure of this visit?" asked Old Boy.

"I was hoping you could tell me about these," said Billy as he pulled out the bottle and showed it to Old Boy; his eyes widened with shock.

"Bloody hell, Billy, where on earth did you get those?!" asked Old Boy.

"Out of Coltan's kit bag," said Billy.

"Ah, I see. He's using it again," said Old Boy.

"I think so," said Billy.

"This is what I'd like your help with. We knew a little of Coltan's addiction because of what he told us, but from my understanding, you were closer with him on the subject," said Billy.

"Coltan's father, Reginald and I grew up together, and he was one of the unfortunates that gave into the addiction of Amphetamines," said Old Boy.

"So, Coltan wasn't the first?" asked Billy.

"You must be joking, Billy. These have been around since the 1880s, and it was only because of the wars or the fear of approaching wars that the army first became interested in them," said Old Boy.

"When they realised how effective Amphetamines were at making their soldiers alert and battle-ready, they made it a mandate that every doctor, medic, and field hospital would carry some", said Old Boy.

"But a few scientists tried to improve the recipe, and the results….were not good," said Old Boy.

"What happened?" asked Billy.

"Turned all the young soldiers' insane, poor souls. So all attempts to improve Amphetamines were scrapped and officially banned," said Old Boy.

"You said Coltan's father was one of the unfortunate ones. How did he become addicted?" asked Billy as Mrs Nesbit walked in with a plate of two chocolate biscuits.

"Here you are, Billy. Both just for you," said Mrs Nesbit as she left the room.

"You're the best, Martha", said Billy as he started to enjoy one of the biscuits; they were his favourite.

"Sorry, carry on," said Billy.

"Reginald and I both signed up during the first war, but we were put in different regiments. Which is why I couldn't stop him from meeting Doctor Hatchet," said Old Boy.

"Doctor Hatchet, I think I've heard that name. Who was he?" said Billy.

"An army doctor in the First World War, and he was convicted in a military court for supplying "Improved" Amphetamines. He was convinced he'd perfected the recipe and didn't know about the side effects," said Old Boy.

"What side effects?" asked Billy.

"Paranoia, delusions, hallucinations, convulsions and death. Reginald came close, but unlike the others, he actually pulled through with treatment. At the cost of losing one of his legs, though," said Old Boy.

"Coltan once told us his father was injured in the last war, but he never said how he lost his leg," said Billy.

"Well, he doesn't like to talk about it, so I won't bring it up either. But suffice to say, Coltan's addiction to these came from his father, and he had hoped it wouldn't happen," said Old Boy.

"So, how is Coltan getting them? Is Doctor Hatchet back?" asked Billy.

"Not much chance of that, I'm afraid, Billy. He died thirty years ago, hung himself in his prison cell with his bed sheets," said Old Boy.

"But I have heard that a few other doctors are trying to "Carry on his work" so to speak. You best be careful, Billy. If Coltan is using these again, he could be placing himself in danger, and not just from death. If he hits the paranoia or hallucination stages in a crowded area....well, you get what I mean," said Old Boy.

"Can I just ask, why are you digging around in Coltan's kit bag?" asked Old Boy.

"I'm just trying to find out how loyal the squad is to each other; we need trust and respect to get through this. If we keep secrets and they come out the hard way, that trust is gone," said Billy, lying through his teeth.

"Well, I agree that trust is important, but rifling through their personal belongings isn't how to keep it. Maybe try to find better ways instead," said Old Boy.

"You're right, Old Boy, I'm sorry," said Billy as he finished the second biscuit.

"Well, I've taken up enough of your time, Old Boy. I best be going," said Billy as he got up; the Old boy did too.

"Yeah, I just need to make a quick phone call to the Home Office before I go to work," said Old Boy.

"What for?" asked Billy, with some slight worry.

"Well, from what you've shown me, these Amphetamine dealers are back, and someone needs to stop them. We don't need a repeat of the last time," said Old Boy.

"Oh, right, of course. Thanks, Old Boy," said Billy as they shook hands.

"Look after yourself, kid, and if Coltan doesn't want to listen to you, send him round to me," said Old Boy.

"Will do", said Billy as he walked out of the living room, said goodbye to Mrs Nesbit and left the house.

He now had to wait for Alice and Lucy to finish school before telling them about his findings.

Sherlock Household, Afternoon, 4:15 pm

Once Alice and Lucy were back at the Sherlock house, Billy showed them the letter and the Amphetamines he'd found connecting to Trevor and Coltan.

"So, let's get this straight. Trevor is having an affair, and Coltan is an addict?" asked Alice.

"Pretty much," said Billy.

"Yeah, you're going to have to help us here," said Lucy.

"Well, Trevor often bragged about this girl he was with back home, Rebecca. A beautiful, sophisticated woman and someone who made him feel like the luckiest guy in the world," said Billy.

"But according to that letter, he's been in some sort of correspondence with a French girl named Michelle," said Billy.

"This letter isn't written in very good English. But it seems she's asking why Trevor stopped writing to her and that she really wants him back," said Lucy.

"And what about these Amphetamines? How long has Coltan been taking them?" asked Alice.

"Well, we never saw him during our first year together, so it must have happened sometime during the second year. And according to Old Boy, Coltan's father was the first to become addicted," said Billy.

"Does any of this help us, Alice?" asked Lucy.

"I think so; these motivate both men to hurt Tyler. He could've threatened to expose Trevor's affair or Coltan's addiction," said Alice.

"That would mean that either of them could've come to Millstone earlier than they said. And hoped to get rid of Tyler to protect their secrets," said Alice.

"What about the gold?" asked Lucy.

"I suppose they felt like helping themselves to the prize for their troubles. But when the letter turned out to be unreadable, they decided to bide their time and wait to see what happens," said Alice.

"So, how do we use this information?" asked Lucy.

"Billy, call Trevor and Coltan and arrange to meet with us at George and Dragon. We'll confront them and try to catch them off guard," said Alice.

"You got it," said Billy as he went to look for the phone.

"You really think that one of them did it?" asked Lucy.

"We will find out soon enough," said Alice.

Chapter 14

Deadly Accusations, Deadly Consequences

<u>George and Dragon Pub, Afternoon, 5:00 pm</u>

Billy called Mr Prosser and asked him to put Trevor or Coltan on the line; when he got a response, he arranged the meeting with them in the pub. But when they both came down the stairs and into the bar, they were surprised to find Billy sitting there at one of the tables with Alice and Lucy.

"Well, this is a surprise; I thought it was just us blokes having a drink," said Trevor.

"I brought some company," said Billy as Coltan and Trevor took their seats.

"So, Billy arranged this meeting because we'd like to ask you both some questions," said Alice as Trevor laughed a bit.

"Well, isn't this precious? The little wannabe investigators would like to interrogate us; you're both so cute," said Trevor.

"Don't call us cute!" said Lucy.

"We're going to show you both some things that are connected to you and then you're going to consider your responses to them carefully. Do you understand?" said Alice.

"Yes sir, anything you say, sir," said Trevor sarcastically with a salute.

Alice pulled out Trevor's letter and handed it to him.

"Do you recognise this letter?" asked Alice as Trevor read it, his eyes widened.

"Where the hell did you get this?" asked Trevor.

"Doesn't matter, do you know what it is?" said Billy.

"My private correspondence is none of your damn business!" said Trevor.

"It just seems strange to us that you have a girlfriend named Rebecca in Millstone, and yet you've been in touch with a French girl named Michelle. You can see how that looks to us," said Alice.

"Look, it's not what you think, okay? Michelle is…..she's in the French Resistance. I met her four years ago when I was in France. We keep in touch so that we can both reassure each other that we're alive and well; she's just a friend, that's all," said Trevor.

"That's a rather forward letter for "Just a friend". All the times she says that she loves you and wants you back, and I don't even need to mention the number of kisses there," said Alice.

"Friends can say they love each other; it's not a crime. When she says she wants me back, she means it is in France; she remembers how much I loved it there. And I mean, come on, she's French after all, so that should explain the kisses without much said," said Trevor.

"Coltan, we have something to show you, too," said Lucy.

"Okay then", said Coltan as Lucy discreetly showed the amphetamine bottle under the table; Coltan's eyes widened.

"Where the hell did you get that?" asked Coltan.

"Same place we got the letter, are they yours?" said Billy.

Coltan didn't want to answer but knew he was backed into a corner.

"You swore to us that you were off them, Coltan" said Billy.

"I did, and I am. It's just….look, I'm not guzzling them like sweets if that's what you think, I just…take one or two every now and then," said Coltan.

"You don't seem surprised, Trevor," said Billy.

"Of course, I'm not. Who the hell do you think has been helping him to keep this a secret?" said Trevor.

"Look, I tried to quit them; I swear I did. But you know what it's like out there; every day on the battlefield brings a whole new trauma that's burned into your mind," said Coltan.

"Soldiers with limbs missing, their hearing blown or trapped in barbed wire, and you want to help them, but you'll die and-Coltan, that's enough!" Billy interrupted Coltan.

"There's kids present," said Billy.

"So then I started to freeze up in the camp; I just couldn't go out there. And I knew the rough teachings the Sergeant can give you to toughen you up, so I went back on them, just to get my confidence up," said Coltan.

"Damn it, Coltan, you know these were banned for a reason. Look at what happened to those soldiers in the last war; these pills will kill you!" said Billy.

"No, I read about those soldiers; they took excessive amounts; I just take one or two, like I said. And before you say it, I'm not letting my Dad down; he did take more than he should have. I'm not going to be like him," said Coltan.

"Okay, enough now. This interrogation has done nothing but bring up embarrassment on both sides. I don't know what game you both are playing, but I'd advise you to stop it," said Trevor.

"Alright, we will skip to the important question. Which one of you stabbed Tyler?" said Alice as Trevor and Coltan were both shocked.

"Say that again, little lady," said Trevor.

"Tyler found out your secrets, didn't he? He threatened to expose you both; that's why you both came here earlier than you claimed and tried to take him out of the picture," said Alice.

"Okay, Alice, you are really crossing the line here. I think you need to stop making such accusations while you still can; you won't like what happens if you don't," said Trevor.

"Don't threaten her, Trevor. You won't like what happens either," said Billy.

"I just meant that I'll tell her parents; calm down, Billy," said Trevor.

"Anyway, Tyler didn't know anything about these things, so you're barking up the wrong tree," said Trevor.

"So you say, but how can you be sure?" said Billy as Trevor was stumped for words now.

"I think it's time we go," said Lucy as everyone got up.

Billy retrieved the letter.

"Hey, that's mine!" said Trevor.

"We'll hold onto it for the time being," said Billy.

"You both know more than you're letting on, and we have too much information and not enough answers. So here's the deal: if neither of you confess about Tyler by tomorrow, we're taking what we've got to the police," said Alice.

"And we mean it, so don't test us," said Lucy as she, Alice and Billy left the bar.

Trevor and Coltan returned to their room.

"Oh, this is bad, this is really bad," said Coltan.

"Calm yourself, Coltan, it's going to be okay," said Trevor.

"Okay?! You saw what happened there; they have incriminating evidence against us. And if we don't tell them what they want to hear, they're going to the police!" said Coltan.

"Well, it will be a bit difficult to convince them otherwise since we don't know anything. But look, what they have is circumstantial at best; it's all theorised, and the police won't pay it any mind," said Trevor.

"That's easy for you to say. You might be able to charm your way out by saying the letter is from a love-crazed French girl, but what about me? When they find out I'm on the Amphetamines, they'll ship me off to the nearest hospital where they'll chemically castrate me!" said Coltan.

"That's only if you're a homosexual unless there's something you're not telling me," said Trevor.

"NO, no, of course not, I'm…I'm straight," said Coltan.

"Look, so long as we stick together and keep our stories straight, we'll be home free....free to return to the front," said Trevor.

"Trevor, they're already trying to pin Tyler's attack on us; what if they try to do the same with Patrick?" said Coltan.

"Patrick's death wasn't our fault," said Trevor.

"You mean it wasn't my fault?" said Coltan.

"Just what is that supposed to mean?" asked Trevor.

"Before Patrick was shot, you went out ahead to recon the area; you swore the way was clear," said Coltan.

"To the best of my knowledge, it was; I don't have a damn radar on my head," said Trevor.

"But when that sniper killed Patrick, his position was covered, but he wasn't well hidden. Even the sun reflected off his scope moments before he fired, so I wonder how you could've missed that," said Coltan.

"You think I deliberately got Patrick killed, that I lured him to his death?!" asked Trevor.

"Maybe, I mean, the less of us there are, the more gold there is to go around," said Coltan.

"And I suppose you're going to try and blame me for Andy's death, too? But the problem with that is I wasn't even in the room, and come to think of it, weren't you supposed to be guarding the Officer?" said Trevor as Coltan seemed deflated.

"Now, I'm not saying it was entirely your fault, but you let an inexperienced young man guard a German Officer who obviously had a trick up his sleeve. So how does that feel?" said Trevor.

Coltan didn't say anything.

"That's what I thought. I'm going out with Rebecca this evening, so you can do whatever you please. But a little advice: don't take those pills, and stay away from the girls," said Trevor as he grabbed his jacket and left the room.

Coltan revealed he had another bottle of Amphetamines hidden away in the room; he poured out two pills, stared at them for a moment, then swallowed them.

Both men were in the spotlight, but Trevor had slightly more confidence than Coltan.

Which one would be the most likely to crack?

Sherlock Household, Evening, 9:30 pm

Lucy returned to her home, as did Billy and Alice. They were contemplating how shady Trevor and Coltan were and whether one of them could've stabbed Tyler. As bedtime came, the house fell asleep, and everything was quiet. That was until the air raid siren started to ring out again, and the sound of planes overhead could be heard.

Everyone ran for the shelter and sealed themselves in. The fact that the shelter was mostly soundproof, aside from the planes, meant that there was one out-of-place noise that they didn't hear further along the coast.

The sound of a gunshot.

Once the air raid had passed, the Sherlocks went back inside and straight to bed, not that they had many hours left before morning. Everyone awoke feeling rather tired, but they had to get themselves ready for the day's events.

A sudden knocking at the door sent Jasper to answer it; he led the person outside into the dining room.

"A police constable, sir," said Jasper.

"Constable, can we help you?" asked Jack.

"Forgive the intrusion to your breakfast, sir, but I'm here to make some enquiries," said the constable.

"But we've told you everything we know about Tyler; we thought the case was closed," said Mavis.

"No, ma'am, it's not about Tyler Sherlock. I'm very sorry to report that a young woman was murdered last night, further along the cliffs from your house," said the constable.

"Oh my goodness, that's horrible," said Mavis.

"I've been sent to interview all nearby residents to see if they saw or heard anything last night," said the constable.

"Excuse me, constable, do you know who the woman is?" asked Alice.

"As it happens, yes. Her sister identified her. Rebecca Hall is her name, a local to Millstone, and very well known," said the constable.

"Oh no, Rebecca, who worked at the ice cream parlour? I think Veronica was friends with her, poor girl,," said Mavis.

"Do you have any idea who might've done it?" asked Alice.

"Actually, we've already arrested a man who was found very close to the murder site and had the weapon in his hand. I believe his army registry card identified him as Trevor Phillips," said the constable as Alice and Billy looked at each other in shock.

They never saw that coming.

The Sherlocks answered what questions they could, but the fact was that they hadn't heard anything while being down in the shelter. Once the constable had left, Billy said he'd walk Alice to school; they caught up with Lucy in the town and told her what had happened.

"Trevor killed his girlfriend?!" asked Lucy.

"That's what the police are saying," said Alice.

"I don't believe it. I know Trevor was being evasive during the interview, but suddenly killing Rebecca out of nowhere? He had no reason to; he loved her," said Billy.

"So the police have locked him up?" asked Lucy.

"Yeah, he's in one of the cells at the station," said Alice.

"I'm going to go and see him once I've dropped you girls off; try and get some answers out of him," said Billy.

"I wish we could go with you, but we can't skip school," said Alice.

"Probably best not to", said Billy as they rounded the corner and were shocked to see part of the school had collapsed and air raid wardens had cordoned off the site.

Billy slowly approached the site with the girls, and they spoke to one of the wardens.

"Excuse me, what happened here?" asked Billy.

"Air raid last night, sir, a bomb landed on the school. No one was inside, thankfully, but it took a chunk out of the building," said the warden.

"The other half looks intact. Are they still allowing classes?" asked Alice.

"Fraid not, miss. We can't allow anyone near until we've done a check for unexploded bombs, and the possibility of radiation from the last one is too risky. Sorry to say, girls, school's cancelled today," said the warden.

Billy looked at the girls.

Do you believe in fate?" asked Billy as Alice and Lucy smiled.

Chapter 15

Sharpshooter

Millstone Police Station, Morning, 9:40 am

Alice, Lucy and Billy made their way to the police station and managed to persuade the sergeant to let them see Trevor. He led them to the cells.

"You've got some visitors, Mr Phillips, for the next ten minutes," said the sergeant as he left the room.

Trevor approached the bars and saw who it was.

"Oh bloody hell, I knew it wouldn't be long before you all came sniffing around again," said Trevor.

"Trevor, I know what you think of us, but I'm here as your friend. I want to believe that this is wrong, but you have to admit, it's pretty bad, mate," said Billy.

"If you really murdered Rebecca, then we're walking out and letting justice take its course. But if there's a chance that you're innocent, like it or not, we may be the only ones who can help you," said Alice.

Trevor gave a big sigh as he knew they were right.

"We're here to listen, mate, just tell us. What the hell happened out there?" said Billy.

"It wasn't my fault, you have to believe me, it wasn't," said Trevor.

"Rebecca and I went out last night; we had a meal in a restaurant and walked around the town a bit like we always did. Then she said that she wanted to walk along the coastline and look at the stars in the sky. I said okay," said Trevor.

"Halfway through the walk, she started to get a little strange," said Trevor.

"What sort of strange?" asked Lucy.

"She started asking questions about our relationship, how strong it was, and our love for each other. I just answered as truthfully as I could, but then she started saying how easy it would be for me to go off with another woman," said Trevor.

"I was about to respond when the air raid siren went off. I went to grab Rebecca so we could run for the nearest shelter, but when I turned around, she'd pulled a gun on me," said Trevor.

"Why would she do that?" asked Alice.

"She found out about Michelle, about the letters and…what we did during that summer four years ago," said Trevor.

"So there was an affair," said Billy.

"Yes, okay, there was. It was in France, but in all fairness, I didn't cheat on Rebecca. We were on a break; we'd just had this massive argument, and both decided that we needed space from each other," said Trevor.

"I met Michelle in Paris, and she was so open and friendly that we ended up having a summer fling. When I came back, we kept in touch by letter, but when Rebecca and I got back together, I sent a final one to Michelle saying that we couldn't talk anymore," said Trevor.

"But Michelle didn't like that, did she?" asked Lucy.

"No, unknowingly, she'd taken our summer fling as a declaration of love. She still sent letters to me saying that she wanted me back, and I burned those letters so that Rebecca wouldn't see them," said Trevor.

"Then how did she find out?" asked Alice.

"I haven't the faintest idea. I know for a fact that she never saw any of the letters. Even that one you've got was hidden in my room, and she never went in there," said Trevor.

"Okay, go back to the coast. What happened?" said Lucy.

"Well, I tried to reason with Rebecca, and she kept going on about how I'd betrayed her and broken her heart. But as one of the planes came over and distracted her, I took my chance and tried to disarm her," said Trevor.

"Then the blasted thing went off, and Rebecca collapsed. I...I didn't mean to shoot her; I swear on my mother's grave, I didn't! I tried to help her, but then the next thing I knew, bang, out went the lights," said Trevor.

"Someone knocked you out?" asked Billy.

"That's what it felt like, and the gash on the back of my head feels it too. When I awoke, a policeman was looking over me and saying I was under arrest. Apparently, I was still holding the gun in my hand," said Trevor.

"Look, I lied to you in the pub about Michelle, I admit that. But I still loved Rebecca, and I didn't mean for her to die, I swear!" said Trevor.

The police sergeant came back in.

"Time's up; you have to go now," said the sergeant.

Everyone left without saying anything to Trevor; he sat back down and tried to contemplate his future.

Alice, Lucy and Billy left the police station.

"Do you think he's telling the truth?" asked Alice.

"I have to admit, this time, he looked really desperate and scared. Not his usual suave and know-it-all all self, no, I'm inclined to believe he was telling the truth," said Billy.

"So he was framed then?" asked Lucy.

"Well, it sounds like he did shoot Rebecca, but it was more an accident. They only think it was murder because he had the gun in his hand and didn't go for help," said Alice.

"So he was knocked out to keep him there and seal his fate as the murderer," said Lucy.

"Someone is out to get the squad. Andy and Patrick's deaths were likely unfortunate casualties, but Tyler, now Trevor. There was planning behind what happened to them," said Alice.

"We have to find Coltan now; he could be next," said Billy as everyone picked up the pace for the George and Dragon pub.

Millstone On Sea Streets, Morning, 10:00 am

Alice, Lucy and Billy made it to the George and Dragon pub and ran inside. Mr Prosser was startled by their entrance.

"Goodness me, what's the hurry?" asked Mr Prosser.

"We need to speak to Coltan, it's urgent, is he here?" said Billy.

"You just missed him. I caught a glimpse of him going out the back door," said Mr Prosser.

"Isn't that a bit strange?" asked Alice.

"No, lots of patrons leave by the back door, don't want their women to see them in the pub", said Mr Prosser as Tim then entered the back door; he seemed confused.

"Everything okay, Tim?" asked Mr Prosser.

"I don't know. Coltan just ran into me out back, nearly knocking me to the ground, and he didn't even stop to say sorry," said Tim.

"How did he look? Did you see his face?" asked Billy.

"Yeah, it was only for a moment, but he looked panicked, frightened for his life," said Tim.

"Do you know which direction he was heading?" asked Lucy.

"Just out into the street from what I saw. And he was carrying something with him; it was covered with a blanket, but it was long and straight," said Tim.

"You don't think...." Alice couldn't finish.

"Come on, we need to search the streets," said Billy as they all headed for the front entrance.

(BANG!)

A loud bang went off as a bullet came through the glass at the front of the pub; everyone ducked down as Billy pulled Alice and Lucy down to the floor. More shots started ringing out as everyone kept low; people in the streets were panicking and running for cover as a policeman was blowing his whistle for assistance. In a bombed-out house at the end of the street, where the gunfire was coming from, crouched down in the room on the second floor and rising up to shoot his rifle, was Coltan.

"STAY THE HELL AWAY FROM ME!!" shouted Coltan as he fired more rounds into the street.

Inside the pub, Billy managed to move Alice and Lucy under one of the tables and told them to keep their heads low. The door suddenly opened as Old Boy came inside, keeping as low as his bones would allow him to.

"Everyone, stay in cover. We have a slight situation, and we'll deal with it as quickly as we can!" said Old Boy as he saw Billy and the girls; he went over to them.

"What are you all doing here?" asked Old Boy.

"Conducting an investigation," said Alice.

"Right," said Old Boy.

"What's happening out there?" asked Billy.

"Someone in that bombed-out house down there is taking pot-shots into the streets. But we can't tell if it's a Nazi or not; he's too dug in," said Old Boy.

"Has anyone been hurt?" asked Lucy.

"Not so far. In fact, whoever it is doesn't appear to be aiming at anyone; he's just firing into the street," said Old Boy.

"Billy, are you thinking what I'm thinking?" asked Alice.

"Stay here," said Billy as he carefully moved up the stairs and into the rooms.

Billy came to the one Coltan, and Trevor was staying in and kicked the door open; he then saw something he'd hoped he wouldn't: a half-empty bottle of Amphetamines. He then made his way back down to the girls and Old Boy.

"I found these," said Billy as he showed the bottle.

"But, I thought we took the only one he had" said Alice.

"He must've had a spare, and it's half empty. If that is Coltan firing out there, he's probably off his rocker," said Billy.

"So what do we do?" asked Lucy.

"Well, once the rest of the Home Guard are in position, they'll try to take him out," said Old Boy.

"But they'll kill him!" said Lucy.

"That's very likely," said Old Boy.

"There must be something we can do!" said Alice.

"I think there is. Mr Prosser, does that back door lead to the street?" said Billy.

"Down the alley? Yeah, it goes to the street," said Mr Prosser.

"Then that gives us one more option. I have to try and talk to Coltan," said Billy.

"But Billy, it's too dangerous; what if he shoots you?" said Alice.

"If I don't do anything, Coltan's going to be killed, and I won't have his death on my conscience. And if he shoots me, then at least I'll die knowing I tried," said Billy.

"Then we're coming with you," said Alice.

"No way, if anything happens to either of you, Tyler and your parents will never forgive me. Trust me, I'll be alright," said Billy.

"Old Boy, you have to get the Home Guard to hold back; if they start shooting, they might kill Billy," said Alice.

"I'll try my best to buy some time, but if they get a clear shot, I don't think I'll be able to stop them from taking it", said Old Boy as he made his way back out the front door.

"Okay, you two stay here, I mean it. If all goes well, I'll be back before you know it," said Billy.

"Billy, wait (Lucy kissed Billy's cheek) for luck", said Lucy as Billy winked at her and started making his way to the back door.

"How did you get into the room upstairs? Did you kick the door down?" asked Tim as Billy passed him.

"Yeah, you might want to consider a renovation. It's very thin wood," said Billy as he made it to the back door.

Once outside, he ran the length of the alley, checked to see which direction Coltan was firing in, then ran to the bombed-out house and climbed the stairs as quietly as he could.

Coltan was still firing a round or two into the street; he had a surprising amount of ammunition. Billy crept into the room and kept a slight distance from him.

"Coltan," said Billy as Coltan turned and aimed his rifle at him.

"Whoa, whoa, Coltan, it's me, it's Billy", said Billy as he could now see his suspicions confirmed.

Coltan's pupils were pinprick small, his breathing was quick, and he was sweating like an animal. These were definite signs of Amphetamine overdose.

"What do you want?!" asked Coltan.

"I'm just here to talk, Coltan, relax," said Billy.

"I'm relaxed, I'm very relaxed, do I not look relaxed?!" said Coltan.

"Coltan, listen to me, you're scaring people. There's panic down there because you're firing bullets into the street!" said Billy.

"It's not like I've hit anyone, and it's not civilians I'm aiming at. It's "Them," said Coltan.

"Who's "Them?" asked Billy.

"THEM! The ones who've been coming after us since we took that gold. Deep down, I had this feeling that we should've left it well alone, and now I know the reason why. It's cursed, Billy, it's goddamn cursed!" said Coltan.

"Coltan, mate, you overdosed on Amphetamines; I think your imagination is running away from you," said Billy.

"NO, NO, IT'S NOT! I'm the only one who's making any sense!" said Coltan.

"Okay, Coltan, I'm sorry; I didn't mean to imply anything. Why do you think the gold is cursed?" said Billy.

"Open your eyes, Billy; think about everything that's happened since we took it. A grenade killed Andy, a sniper shot Patrick, Tyler was stabbed on his home turf, and now Trevor is in jail for killing his girlfriend. He says he didn't do it, but you know what? I DON'T BELIEVE HIM!" said Coltan, shouting the last bit.

"Coltan, please listen to me, mate. This isn't you; it's not you thinking this; the overdose has messed with your head," said Billy.

"Billy, you have to see it; I can't be the only one. Someone or something is coming after us all; it's revenge because we took the gold!" said Coltan.

"Okay, then how about this? Let's turn the gold in, all of it, to the Home Office. It might be that whatever's after us wants the right thing to be done. Maybe it'll all be better once it's done," said Billy.

"No, you don't get it. We can't turn in the gold because.....I don't know where it is!" said Coltan.

"What do you mean?" asked Billy.

"I sent a letter to my smuggler friend before we came over and told him to forward the next one to Millstone. But when I didn't hear anything, I got in touch with a contact of his who lived nearby," said Coltan.

"The letter I got back told me that the Nazis raided his hideout and captured him. He hasn't been seen or heard from since. But one thing that was made certain, the Nazis turned the hideout upside down, and they didn't find the gold there," said Coltan.

"So now it's lost; no one knows where it is. We can't turn it in, we can't do the right thing, we're screwed, Billy!" said Coltan.

"Coltan, please listen to what I'm saying. There is no curse; all that's happened is many unfortunate and tragic life losses. But it's not the work of some mythical being or spirit; it's all in your head, Coltan, that's all it is," said Billy.

"Oh god, you're right; of course you're right," said Coltan.

"You see. Now, why don't you give me the rifle, and we'll walk out of here, okay?" said Billy, but Coltan seemed deep in thought.

"How could I have been so stupid? I should've seen it," said Coltan.

"Trust me, mate, it's easily done," said Billy.

"It's me; it's always been me," said Coltan.

"Wait, what?" asked Billy.

"You said it wasn't a mythical being or spirit because, in actuality, it's been a mortal man. It's me, I did this!" said Coltan.

"Coltan, you're letting your imagination run away with you again," said Billy.

"I was the first one to touch the gold; that's how it took hold of me," said Coltan.

"Coltan, listen to me," said Billy.

"I was supposed to be the one guarding the Officer, but I gave it to Andy, and he got killed. And I saw the sniper scope glimmering in the sun, but I didn't warn Patrick, and he got killed," said Coltan.

"Coltan, stop this!" said Billy.

"I had a blackout in the camp. Trevor just said I was asleep for a few hours, but what if it was for a few days?" said Coltan.

"I could have left without anyone realising, came here and stabbed Tyler with my bayonet and gone back before roll call," said Coltan.

"Coltan, that's impossible," said Billy.

"And I took some pills when Trevor went out. I must've followed him and set him up for murder; it's all coming together now!" said Coltan.

"Coltan, please, I'm begging you to stop this; you don't know what you're saying!" said Billy.

"I did this, it's always been me, and I didn't know…..I didn't…..well, now I do know," said Coltan as he suddenly aimed the rifle under his chin.

"Coltan, don't!" said Billy.

"Tell my father I'm sorry, I'm sorry I let him down!" said Coltan as he went to pull the trigger.

Billy leapt forward and grabbed the rifle, jerking it to the right as it went off.

The two of them struggled until Billy head-butted Coltan, making him let go of the rifle and hit him in the face with it. Coltan fell to the floor, dazed from the hit; Billy threw down the rifle and waved a white handkerchief to signal that it was over. The Home Guards called out to each other and started moving in.

Coltan was now crying in a curled-up position.

"Why…why didn't you let me do it?!" asked Coltan.

"I've lost enough friends already; I won't lose anymore," said Billy as the Home Guards burst into the room with Old Boy.

"It's okay; he's down," said Billy.

"I'm sorry Andy....I'm so sorry, kid," said Coltan as he kept crying his eyes out.

"Bring in the stretcher," said Old Boy. As a stretcher was brought in, Coltan was loaded on and carried away.

Billy breathed a sigh of great relief as Old Boy put his hand on his shoulder.

"That was a very brave thing you did, son, you probably saved his life," said Old Boy.

"Yeah, but is it a life he'll get back?" said Billy as Old Boy didn't say anything.

He didn't know what to say.

Chapter 16

Focus the Mind

Millstone Hospital, Morning, 11:20 am

Coltan was taken to hospital and had a stomach pump to drain his system. Alice, Lucy and Billy were in the waiting area until the same doctor treating Tyler came through the doors, along with the police sergeant and Old Boy.

"How is he, doc?" asked Billy.

"Well, he seems to be over the worst of it. The stomach pump has made him get most of it out of his system; now, of course, he's got a terrible headache and has been asking what's for dinner," said the Doctor.

"The tests show this is definitely an Amphetamine overdose, but we've dealt with this before; we know what to do," said the Doctor.

"Are you going to arrest him, Sergeant?" asked Alice.

"I'm afraid I have to. Despite that no one got hurt, Mr Strand still fired into a crowded street and terrorised a lot of people," said the Sergeant.

"But, since it was an overdose, can't you see that he gets treatment for it instead of locking him up?" asked Lucy.

"Well, with the doctor's report, we're hoping it'll be enough for the judge to go easy on Mr Strand. And yes, hopefully, we can push for treatment rather than prison," said the Sergeant.

"Old Boy told me what you did, young man; you were very brave," said the Sergeant.

"I've seen too many people I know die in this terrible war; I won't lose anymore if I can help it," said Billy.

"Good man," said the Sergeant.

"Speaking of which. Miss Sherlock, I was going to call your parents, but maybe you can pass them a message for me?" said the Doctor.

"Is it about Tyler?" asked Alice.

"It is. Well, you can tell your parents…..that they don't need to worry about making funeral arrangements," said the Doctor with a smile.

"Wait, you mean….Tyler's alive?!" asked Alice.

"He is. The surgery was touch and go for a while, but Tyler is stronger than he looks. He pulled through, we stopped the bleeding, and now we're confident that he's going to fully recover in the given time," said the Doctor, as Alice looked like she was about to cry.

Lucy hugged her, and Billy hugged both of them.

"Thank you, Doctor. Can we see him?" said Alice.

"I'm sorry, Alice, but we still need to keep Tyler in a coma and give his body a chance to heal before he can move around. But once he can wake up, I'll let you know," said the Doctor.

"Now, if you'll excuse me, I need to check on our new patient," said the Doctor as he walked away.

"I'll come with you," said the Sergeant.

"I don't need a police escort, Sergeant," said the Doctor.

"Can't be too careful, sir?" said the Sergeant as they both walked away.

"Did you find out how he got the rifle?" Alice asked Old Boy.

"Yeah, I did. One of the privates in the Home Guard said his house was broken into, and his rifle was stolen. And he lives right next door to the pub," said Old Boy.

"Speaking of which, I'd better return this to him," said Old Boy as he left, carrying the rifle.

"I wonder where Coltan got all the ammunition to fire into the street," said Lucy.

"Something tells me his smuggler friend may have been helping him to stockpile some. He must have brought it with him," said Billy.

"Do you believe his confession?" asked Alice.

"I believe he blames himself for Andy and Patrick's deaths. But when he was trying to connect himself to stabbing Tyler and framing Trevor, no, it didn't make any sense," said Billy.

"And I take it that the gold is no longer a motive?" asked Lucy.

"Well, it may still be on the table. But Coltan sounded sincere when he told me that he doesn't know where the gold is, not since the Germans captured the smuggler," said Billy.

"Which does pose a problem. We can't collect our share, and we also can't turn it in, basically like Coltan said, we're screwed," said Billy.

"But on the bright side, Tyler is on his way to recovery. That must be a weight off your shoulders, Alice," said Lucy.

"Yeah, it really is. But I still have one weight, and it's that we still haven't found Tyler's attacker yet. He might try again if he finds out Tyler's alive," said Alice.

"Well, Alice, I hate to admit it, but we're out of options. We've exhausted all our leads and reached a dead end," said Lucy.

"I'm afraid she's right. We've been through everyone left on the squad, and we can't connect any of them to Tyler. There's no one else we can look at," said Billy.

"So, it's over then?" asked Lucy.

"It looks that way," said Alice as she got up.

"Alice, I didn't mean to upset you," said Lucy.

"No, it's okay, Lucy, you haven't. I just need some air; I'll be back in a minute," said Alice as she stepped outside the hospital.

Alice stood there for a moment until a familiar voice suddenly appeared next to her.

"Is the case concluded then?" asked Sherlock Holmes.

"Mr Holmes, I was hoping that you were going to show up; I really need your help," said Alice.

"So it appears, it seems that the element of doubt has once again crept its way into you," said Sherlock.

"Please believe me, Mr Holmes. It's not that I want to give up this time, but we've run out of things to look at; we've checked all our leads and clues. It's basically like Lucy said, we're at a dead end," said Alice.

"Alice, do you know how many times Watson and I have hit dead ends during our cases? We've definitely had our fair share. Some have been tiring and frustrating, and a few have even pinned us against each other," said Sherlock.

"Which is why I'm keen to remind my dear friend that there's always one place left to check. A place that always has information and never runs out," said Sherlock as he pointed at his head.

"My mind? But there's so much in there; a lot of it is jumbled," said Alice.

"Alice, you've read my books. What's the one thing I like doing when I really need to think hard and deep?" said Sherlock.

"Don't you call it your brain attic?" asked Alice.

"That's what you need to do, Alice. Go deep into your brain attic, focus everything you know about the case and search for an answer because it's in there; you just have to find it," said Sherlock.

"Yeah, you're right, thanks Mr....Holmes," said Alice as she turned to see that he'd already disappeared.

Alice found there was a bench just a short distance from the hospital, most likely if the waiting area was full. She walked over, sat down cross-legged, closed her eyes and began to focus her mind.

Alice thought about everything that had happened from the moment Tyler came home, the fight in the pub, the stabbing, and learning about the gold and the pact that protected the squad from each other. She listed what she knew about everyone.

Coltan Strand, Amphetamine addict and paranoid.

Trevor Phillips is prideful and a cheat.

Andy Walker is dead.

Patrick Regan is also dead.

Billy Desmond is a trustworthy friend and companion but a liar.

Tyler Sherlock is a loving brother who cares for his family but is also a liar.

Alice then thought about what she'd heard in conversations, things that didn't seem relevant but maybe something now, and one thing stuck to her mind. The gold, the Germans and something Billy had said about frequent air raids.

Alice opened her eyes and gasped; she had it.

"The Germans!" said Alice as she raced back into the waiting area.

"What, are they here?!" asked Billy as he jumped up.

"No, that's the missing link; it's the connection we've been looking for!" said Alice as Billy and Lucy looked at each other.

"Yeah, you've lost us, Alice," said Lucy.

"Billy, you said that when you stole that gold, you'd heard rumours about Hitler hiding bits of his private reserves in other countries," said Alice.

"Yeah," said Billy.

"And recently, you said that air raids on Millstone had increased over time," said Alice.

"Yeah, I did," said Billy.

"Well, that's the whole point; it's the only thing that makes sense," said Alice.

"Okay, Alice, you're not making any sense. Just slow down and tell us what you want to say," said Lucy.

"Hitler wants his gold back, and he knows that a group of British soldiers took it. But he can't just stroll into British territory and get it back, so he resorts to another method, a more...hidden method," said Alice as Lucy began to catch on.

"The spy, the one who they think is signalling the air raids, he's after the gold!" said Lucy.

"Yes, or at least a clue as to how to find it. That's what all the air raids are for; it's the one time when all the houses in town are empty because everyone is down in the shelters," said Alice.

"So then he gets to rifle through the homes, presumably connected to the squad members who recently returned, and try to find a clue to the gold!" said Lucy as she and Alice started jumping up and down with excitement.

"Okay, girls, I love jumping and smiling, but I have a question. These extra air raids have been happening for almost a month, and Tyler and I didn't come back until a week ago. How do you explain that?" asked Billy.

"Also, why would the spy risk exposing himself by trying to kill Tyler?" asked Billy.

"I admit there's still some holes, but it's the best lead we have left. We need to find this spy and get the answers out of him," said Alice.

"Which poses another problem, Alice. How the heck do we find a German spy?" said Lucy as Billy snapped his fingers.

"I know just the man who will help us," said Billy.

Nesbit (Old Boy) House, Afternoon, 12:00 pm

Alice, Lucy and Billy went round to see Old Boy; he'd gone home as his wife always cooked lunch for him. He wasn't too happy about the disruption as it was just coming out of the oven but was more interested when the girls said they needed to find the spy, and thankfully, he had some leads.

Old Boy led them into the attic, where he kept a lot of his old wartime gear and uniform and a map of the town he had been using to try and find the spy. He laid the map on a table and opened it up.

"As you can see, I've done a rather thorough investigation into all these houses and areas which have decent vantage points for signalling to aircraft," said Old Boy.

"And I'm guessing by all the crosses that none of them have worked out?" asked Alice.

"Unfortunately not. Each one of them had the same problem: not enough places to hide and conceal yourself. And Nazi spies love to hide in plain sight and make us look like idiots," said Old Boy.

"What about this house down here, the one with the circle?" asked Lucy.

"That's the final place I haven't got round to checking yet. It's a boarding house off of Chippen Street. Miss Fox runs the place, and she has a few long-term residents," said Old Boy.

"So why haven't you looked there yet?" asked Billy.

"I suppose I'm worried that it's not going to work out like all the others. I'm tired of going from one place to the next, and that spy is no doubt laughing at me from the perfect hiding spot," said Old Boy.

"Well, no offence to you, Old Boy, but maybe you might have better luck with a fresh set of eyes and ears", said Alice as Old Boy was about to respond, but Billy stopped him.

"I know what you're thinking, and all I can say is, don't bother. You can't talk them out of it once their minds are made up. Believe me, I've tried," said Billy.

Old Boy looked at the girls, who smiled at him, and he smiled back.

"Well, I could really do with the assistance. These air raids are becoming more frequent, and if this spy keeps helping them to bomb houses and drop incendiaries, Millstone may not survive the year," said Old Boy.

"Alright then, we'll go tonight. If there's going to be another air raid, hopefully, we can stop it," said Old Boy.

"Very well, we'll come and meet you at the boarding house. What time?" said Billy.

"Better make it 8:00 pm once I've put the wife to bed," blurted Old Boy as Mrs Nesbit appeared by the stairs.

"Andrew, your lunch is going cold," said Mrs Nesbit.

"Coming now, dear," said Old Boy.

"Are you going to ask your friends to stay? There's plenty to go around," said Mrs Nesbit.

"Stay for lunch?" Old Boy asked the others.

"We'd love to", said Alice as everyone headed back down the stairs to enjoy some of Mrs Nesbit's famous cottage pie.

Chapter 17

To Catch A Spy

<u>Miss Fox's Boarding House, Evening, 8:00 pm</u>

As the night descended on the town, everything was surprisingly quiet. So far, the siren hadn't gone, which meant that Alice and the others still had time to search the final house for the spy. Maybe they could prevent any further damage or loss of life, but that would only be if it worked out.

Everyone approached the front door of the boarding house, and Old Boy was the first to knock. It was opened shortly after by Miss Fox, a woman in her late fifties.

"Old Boy, I didn't expect to see you here. Do you know what time it is?" said Miss Fox.

"Forgive me, Miss Fox, but we'd like to search your boarding house for signs of a German spy," said Old Boy.

"A German spy? Here? Have you been feeling unwell lately, Old Boy?" asked Miss Fox.

"Miss Fox, it's really important that we look around inside. We won't take or disturb anything, but we really need to check this place, then we'll leave you alone," said Alice.

"Normally, I don't appreciate people waking up my residents to search their rooms in the middle of the night; I tend to send those people on their way", said Miss Fox.

"But, as you have Alice and Lucy with you, and I still remember how they saved me from looking like an idiot and losing this house, I'll let you in", said Miss Fox as she invited everyone into the main lobby.

"Um, what did you girls do for Miss Fox?" asked Billy.

"She thought that one of her previous residents was a Fifth Columnist, so she asked us to investigate him," said Lucy.

"And it's a good thing they did before I called the police. It turns out the man was a foreign diplomat disguised to hide his presence. It didn't help that he had a craggy jaw, and his eyes were too close together," said Miss Fox.

"Okay, Miss Fox, the sooner we can search the rooms, the sooner your residents can get back to sleep," said Old Boy.

"Well then, let's make a start," said Miss Fox.

Miss Fox began to show Alice, Lucy, Billy and Old Boy around the house, waking up the disgruntled residents who weren't too happy to be pulled from their beds. But nothing had been found after checking four out of the five rooms.

"Okay, just one more room to go. Whose is it?" said Old Boy.

"That'll be Mr Morgan; his room is down the corridor on the right", said Miss Fox as everyone was about to head in that direction, but an all too familiar sound rang through the air.

"The siren, damn it, we're too late!" said Old Boy.

"Never mind that let's get everyone to the shelter; where is it?" said Billy.

"The basement, let's go," said Miss Fox as everyone ran downstairs to the lobby.

A few of the residents on the same floor followed and headed for the basement.

The sounds of planes could be overheard.

"Oh blimey O'Reilly, they're already over the town," said Billy as a loud explosion was heard from outside.

Old Boy opened the front door and looked outside.

"Oh bloody hell, they've dropped a stick of incendiaries down the street! I need to get out there, Billy; come with me, we'll need the help!" said Old Boy.

"Girls, you stay here. Help Miss Fox get everyone into the basement and stay there; we'll be back as quickly as we can," said Old Boy as he and Billy dashed out the door.

Alice and Lucy helped to guide the other residents into the basement; they even helped one of the more elderly ones when she was slowing down a bit.

"Let us help you, Miss," said Lucy.

"Oh, thank you, girls, you're very kind," said the lady as they got her to the basement entrance.

"Okay, is that everyone? Wait, I don't remember seeing Mr Morgan," said Miss Fox.

"I saw him go into his room an hour ago, and as memory serves, he hasn't come back out since," said the lady.

"Miss Fox, get into the basement; we'll find Mr Morgan," said Alice.

"No girls, it's too dangerous," said Miss Fox.

"We'll be okay. We'll head up, find Mr Morgan and be back in two shakes of a lamb's tail," said Alice.

"Oh, okay then. But if his room is locked and he doesn't answer, you'll need the key here," said Miss Fox as she handed them the room key.

"Now hurry up and be careful", said Miss Fox as Alice and Lucy ran upstairs. She then went into the basement and closed the door behind her.

"Those two are very brave," said the lady.

Alice and Lucy arrived upstairs and ran to the room at the end of the hall; they started knocking loudly and calling out.

"Mr Morgan, are you in there?!" cried Alice.

"Mr Morgan, there's an air raid; we have to go to the basement!" cried Lucy, but no one replied.

Alice got out the key and started to unlock the door.

"Mr Morgan, we're coming in!" said Alice as they opened the door and went inside.

The room wasn't very big, just a bed, a chest, a window and a large bookcase.

"There's no one here. But why was the door locked?" said Lucy.

Alice started to think as she approached the bookcase; she started moving the books before placing them back.

"What are you doing?" asked Lucy.

"Following a hunch," said Alice as she moved the books.

Lucy caught sight of a picture of a man; it looked familiar.

"Alice, I think this looks like-" Before Lucy could finish, Alice moved another book and felt something click.

The bookcase moved to one side and revealed a hidden room.

Inside that room was another desk with a radio set and a code machine on it. Alice and Lucy looked to see a man sitting in the chair, talking in German on the radio. The man turned, and shock filled the girl's face.

It was Tim from the George and Dragon pub.

"Tim?" said Alice with surprise.

Tim didn't say anything; he removed the headphones and looked at what the girls saw as a gun on the desk. Alice and Lucy started stepping backwards.

"Tim, don't do this," said Alice.

"Please, Tim, don't hurt us," said Lucy.

Tim seemed to think for a moment.

"God forgives me," said Tim as he reached for the gun.

Alice and Lucy legged it out of the room as he fired a shot that missed them and hit the wall.

They reached the front door and tried to open it, but it wouldn't.

"It's stuck!" said Lucy as they kept pulling on it.

Tim started coming down the stairs as Alice and Lucy ran through the lobby and into the kitchen.

They ducked down by one of the cupboards and tried to remain silent. Tim entered the kitchen and started looking around; he knew they were there. But as he turned around, Alice suddenly threw a plate that hit him in the face and dazed him a bit. They ran for the door again, and he quickly chased after them. They forced open the door and headed outside, but Tim was able to grab Lucy as they did.

"LET GO OF HER!!" shouted Alice as she jumped on Tim's back.

Lucy struggled to break free of his grip, but he let go, allowing her to fall to the ground. Then, he grabbed Alice and threw her down, too.

"This isn't what I wanted....God, believe me, it isn't!" said Tim.

"Tim, please, you don't have to do this!" said Alice.

"I'm so sorry!" said Tim as he aimed to shoot.

"(BANG) ARGH!!" suddenly shouted Tim as a shot went off and knocked the gun from his hand, even taking a couple of fingers with it.

Alice and Lucy looked and saw with relief that Old Boy had fired the shot.

Billy came running up with several Home Guards behind him; they grabbed and restrained Tim, and even their Captain was there.

"Now, would someone tell me what the hell is happening here? Why are you two girls outside?

Don't you know there's an air raid on?!" asked the Captain.

"Sir, Tim is a German spy; his room's radio set and code machine confirm it. The second floor at the end on the right," said Lucy.

"Check it out, Corporal," said the Captain as the Corporal ran inside.

A few moments later, he came back.

"It's all there, sir, just like the girls said," said the Corporal as the Captain approached Tim.

"Well, do you have anything to say for yourself?" asked the Captain as Tim looked at him.

"Heil Hitler," said Tim.

"Get him out of my sight," said the Captain as the Home Guards led Tim away.

"And get these girls into a shelter; the air raid isn't over yet!" said the Captain as he left.

"Thanks, Old Boy," said Alice.

"No problem, now come on, let's get you into the basement", said Old Boy as everyone went back inside.

They certainly had a lot to talk about.

Millstone Police Station, Evening, 10:50 pm

The air raid finally ended when a squadron of Spitfires chased off the German planes, and without their spy to coordinate the attack, they retreated. Despite a number of incendiaries being dropped, the fires they created had been brought under control. Millstone had been saved.

Alice, Lucy, and Billy were brought to the police station and learned quite a lot about the simple barman known as Tim, who wasn't even his name; it was difficult to pronounce, but his first name was Jurgen. According to the information in the radio and code machine, Tim was implanted in Millstone almost a year ago; his orders were to get to know the town and gain the trust of the population, then he'd sign up with the Home Guard and learn their defence plans which he would send to Germany. But after Tyler and his squad stole the gold, his orders changed, and he was to find any evidence among the men about where the gold was being kept if they returned to Millstone. Alice was also right; the extra air raids were done so he could search the houses of the men who came back, but he failed.

Old Boy came to see them in the reception area after he'd interrogated Tim for a while.

"How did it go? Did he say anything else?" asked Alice.

"Not much. One thing about the Germans is that they're very good at training their spies to stay quiet. But I've had my own training to get under their skin," said Old Boy.

"Of course, I'm still not officially military, so the army is sending an armed escort to pick him up and take him for further interrogation elsewhere," said Old Boy.

"However, there is one matter to clear up. Tim said something rather worrying about gold and Tyler," said Old Boy as worry hit everyone.

"Does anyone else know about it?" asked Billy.

"No, fortunately for you, my former army position means I'm still trusted to interrogate Nazi spies solo. And I convinced the police that the mention of gold in the code machine was a deliberate attempt to distract us, so they've ignored those sections, and I'll tell the army the same," said Old Boy.

"Now, I don't know if there's any truth to what he said, and frankly, I don't want to know. But just remember, if that's the case and this gets out, you'll be bringing me down too, you understand?" said Old Boy.

"We get it, Old Boy, we're very appreciative of this," said Billy.

"If I were you, I'd start thinking about how to make things right," said Old Boy.

"Believe me, Old Boy, we're trying really hard", said Billy as the Chief Inspector appeared and came over.

"Well, Mr Jurgan has taken a vow of silence, so to speak. All we can do now is keep him locked up until the armed escort gets here," said the Chief.

"Now then, Miss Sherlock, Miss Porter, I understand that Millstone is thankful to the both of you for exposing Tim as the spy under our noses," said the Chief.

"Thank you, Chief, but in all honesty, it was Old Boy who led the way, so any credit should go to him," said Alice.

"Yeah, he's been on the case since the start and saved our lives," said Lucy.

"Well then, Millstone is also thankful to you, Old Boy. It seems you finally relieved that military glory you've been searching for all this time," said the Chief.

"Thank you, Chief, I live to serve my country," said Old Boy.

"Well, come into my office, and we'll put it in writing," said the Chief as he walked away with Old Boy, who gave the girls a silent "Thank you" as he did.

"So, is that it? The case is over?" asked Lucy.

"Well, Tim has the best possible motive for going after Tyler and the others to get the gold back for Germany. I guess all we can do now is let the army do their thing and get him to confess," said Alice.

"I just...I can't believe it's over. We finally got him," said Billy.

"I said we would, and I always keep my promises," said Alice.

"You know, I dug out this old picture; it was taken in the camp (Billy pulls out a darkened picture of the squad in their army gear). That's Tyler and me; there's Andy Walker, God rest him, and Patrick Regan, too, God rest him. Then there's Trevor Phillips and Coltan Strand," said Billy.

"Until that business with the gold, we were inseparable. The best squad in the army and practically best friends" said Billy.

"It'll be okay, Billy. It may take time, but it'll all be okay," said Alice.

"I really wish I had your confidence," said Billy as Mavis and Jack suddenly came rushing in.

"Alice!" said Mavis as she ran over and hugged her tightly.

"I don't know whether to kiss you or slap you. What were you thinking, you silly girl?!" said Mavis.

"I'm really sorry, Mum, I was just helping. I didn't mean to make you mad," said Alice.

"Right now, I'm too proud to be mad, and I'm just glad you're safe," said Mavis.

"So am I," said Jack as he hugged Alice too.

"You did great for Millstone, Alice, and we're very proud of you. But maybe try not to do it again anytime soon," said Jack.

"I'll try not to," said Alice.

"Now come on, it's very late. There may not be school at the moment, but it doesn't mean you can stay up past your bedtime," said Mavis.

"Just give me a minute," said Alice as she approached Billy and Lucy.

"You'll come round tomorrow, right Lucy?" asked Alice.

"Of course, we'll go searching for our next big case," said Lucy as she and Alice hugged.

"I'll be back at the house soon once I've walked Lucy home. Not that a hug wouldn't be nice, too," said Billy. Alice laughed and hugged him.

Alice then left with her parents and went home; it would seem that the big case had ended.

All they could do now was wait for the next day to start afresh.

Chapter 18

The Truth is Revealed

Sherlock Household, Midnight, 12:00 pm

The Sherlocks returned home, and soon enough, they'd all settled down in their beds and be fast asleep. However, Alice couldn't help going into her brain attic while she slept; something just felt wrong, and something was out of place. They'd found Tim, and he had a motive with the gold as the prize, but thinking about it, he didn't seem to fit the picture completely. Alice started to have another deep and hard think about everything they knew, and after a moment, she woke up and gasped.

"It wasn't Tim; he didn't do it, any of it", said Alice as she pulled herself from bed and sneaked over to Billy's room, knocking on the door quietly as she opened it.

"Billy, Billy, we need to talk", said Alice quietly as she went into the room and found Billy wasn't there; his bed hadn't even been slept in.

Thinking about it, Alice knew there was only one other place he could be. She sneaked back to her room, put on some clothes, tiptoed down the stairs to the front door, put on her coat and shoes, and quietly left. Once outside, she ran all the way down to the beachfront where Billy's cave was. She arrived at the rocky pathway and saw that the tide was starting to come in. She carefully stepped on the stones, trying not to slip and fall in, and made it to the other side.

"Billy, are you here?" called Alice as she stepped into the cave.

"Billy!" said Alice as she ran further in after noticing Billy lying on the ground.

She knelt down next to him; he was still breathing but seemed to be unconscious.

"Billy, Billy, can you hear me?" said Alice as she stopped when she heard something.

It took her a moment to realise it was the click of a gun.

"No, the short answer is he can't hear you," said a voice from a short distance behind her.

"Now stand up and turn around," said Alice's voice as she slowly got up and turned, her eyes widened with shock.

"Oh my goodness!" said Alice as she looked at the person standing there, and couldn't believe her eyes.

She was looking at the face of a dead man.

"I know you from the photograph. You're Andy Walker, the soldier who died," said Alice.

"You mean the soldier who was betrayed by his brothers and left to die in enemy territory? Then yes, you're right," said Andy.

Andy didn't look much like his old self. His face was covered in scars with signs that they'd been stitched up, his right eye was bloodshot, and both of his hands were lightly bandaged.

"But that's impossible. Tyler said you'd died; a grenade killed you," said Alice.

"And yet, here I am (cough) (cough) (strained breathing). My bones only just back together, and I feel like death every time I breathe, but I guess that's what grenades and Nazi hospitality do to you," said Andy.

"What happened to you out there, Andy? What did the Nazis do to you?" asked Alice.

"Why do you care? You wouldn't understand," said Andy.

"Then help me understand," said Alice.

"When that grenade went off, and I felt the burning sensation across my body, I thought that I would just be gone, disintegrated. But instead, I woke up in a German field hospital; they were really happy I'd survived; they finally had someone to torture," said Andy.

"They gave me a rough patch up, and the torture began a few days later. They asked me all sorts of questions about troop movements, Britain's defences and the state of its leadership. And like the good soldier I was, I told them nothing," said Andy.

"Every day I was there, I held out hope that my squad would come bursting in to rescue me. But you know what? They never did; they'd abandoned me, left me to die," said Andy.

"That's not true. Tyler and the others thought you'd died in that house," said Alice.

"THEN WHY DIDN'T THEY COME BACK FOR ME?! WHY DIDN'T THEY TRY TO RECOVER MY BODY, AND REALISE I WAS MISSING?!!" shouted Andy as he coughed and breathed with strain.

Alice didn't respond; she didn't know how to.

"Exactly. The truth of it is that Tyler knew I was trying to dissuade the rest of the squad from keeping the gold, that we should just hand it in. Deep down, I knew that he would find a way to make sure I had an "accident" and clear the way for the squad to have their riches," said Andy.

"How did you get back?" asked Alice.

"Towards the end of the third week, I'd just about given up hope of being rescued; I just wanted them to kill me. But then, the door opened, and I couldn't believe who it was standing there, Adolph Hitler himself," said Andy.

"At that moment, I thought about making my death one to be mentioned posthumously, "The man who killed Adolph Hitler and ended the war". But instead, he offered me a mission: to recover the stolen gold and punish the thieves who took it, my former brothers," said Andy.

"It was you; it's been you this whole time. Going after the squad, one by one," said Alice.

"Oh, you are a good detective, Alice. With the support of German resources, it was easy to get around. Patrick was the first direct hit in the chest with a sniper, and he never saw it coming," said Andy.

"I didn't intend for Tyler to get hurt yet; I just wanted the letter in his coat. But he caught onto my presence, so I had to act quickly," said Andy.

"Trevor was easy, too; I knew all about his affair with the French girl. That's why I took one of his letters and sent it to Rebecca. You see, she was supposed to kill him in a crime of passion, but when he turned it around, it just made it all the more fun to frame him," said Andy.

"And Coltan, he was the best of all of them. Already paranoid and jittery because of those Amphetamines, it didn't take much to fill him with so much fear that he took more than he usually did," said Andy.

"What about Tim? Were you both working together?" asked Alice.

"Sort of, yes. Tim was under orders to infiltrate the Home Guard when he'd built enough trust, but it was taking too long. So Germany ordered him to do the extra air raids to test the town's response and pave the way for an invasion," said Andy.

"But then I came along, and the last few were so I could search the houses or residences of my former squad. I actually broke into yours as well at one point; you really have a fascination for Sherlock Holmes; no wonder you think you're just like him," said Andy as he coughed and breathed with strain.

235

"Tell me what it is you want, just leave Billy alone," said Alice.

"What I want is revenge, Alice, for being forgotten by my friends, my brothers. What you ask is a lot, but I may be able to accept it if you answer one question for me. Where is the gold?" said Andy.

"And what happens if I tell you? What's Hitler offering you in return, money?" asked Alice.

"No, he's offering me something more important than money, something that a lot of those young soldiers like me would kill for. Freedom is a ticket out of this war and over to the winning side," said Andy.

"Surely you must realise, Alice, Britain cannot win the war. Germany is too powerful; they can't be beaten this time," said Andy.

"So you'll just bring them the gold and run away like a coward," said Alice.

"Well, it's not like I can do anything with it! Look at me; do you see what's been done to me? If I took off this uniform, and you saw the second-degree burns I have, you'd probably faint!" said Andy.

"I'll never get married or have children. All I can do is get as far away from the war as possible and rest in my final days," said Andy.

"Final days? You're dying?" asked Alice.

Andy coughed and breathed with strain before he answered.

"Won't last the year since you're so interested. Now I believe that I asked you a question. Where is the gold? Tell me!" said Andy as he got really close to Alice and put the gun in her face.

"I'm not scared of you," said Alice.

"I'd believe it if you weren't so obviously shaking. Where is it? Where's the gold hidden?!" said Andy.

Alice was shivering and almost couldn't speak, but then she did.

"I don't know," said Alice.

"You know, I really thought that we'd reached an understanding, Alice. You see, I've wanted to kill you for days now for poking your nose in, asking questions and drawing attention. I should've been out of here by now, but you just couldn't let it go, could you?" said Andy.

"Now, make this bit easier for me. Just close your eyes and wait for the bang," said Andy.

"It's a little difficult to focus when your hand is bleeding," said Alice.

"It is?" said Andy as he turned to look.

Alice then kicked his ankle and hit him in the face as hard as she could. Andy fell into a pool of water next to them; he played around a bit while Alice legged it out of the cave.

Alice tried to go back the way she came, but the tide was further in and had covered the pathway. The only other way Alice could go was further along the cliffs and look for another way up, so she started moving, splashing through the water as she did. Andy was able to pull himself from the pool, and after regaining his composure, he took off after Alice, quickly realising which way she'd gone, but he did not notice that he'd forgotten to pick up his gun.

Alice kept moving along the cliffs, but she started sinking into the wet sand as she tried to go further after turning a corner. Alice had to think fast before getting stuck; only one option came to mind: she started to climb the cliff, just grabbing onto the rocks and pulling herself up. Andy rounded the corner moments later and looked around; he then looked up and saw Alice; he smiled and went for his gun, only then realising he didn't have it. He cursed himself and started to climb the cliff, too. Alice had a good head start, but despite Andy's injuries, he was slightly quicker. Alice tried to go as fast as she could, but just as she was within reach of the top, Andy grabbed hold of her ankle and stopped her.

"Where is the gold?!" shouted Andy.

"I don't know!" Alice shouted back as Andy started to pull on her ankle.

"Tell me, or I'll pull you off this cliff!!" shouted Andy.

"Where is my gold?!" shouted Andy.

"It's not yours! You're just giving it back to the Germans!" shouted Alice.

"And they're giving me my freedom to be as far away from this unwinnable war as possible!" shouted Andy.

"Now, for the final time of asking. WHERE. IS. THE GOLD?!!" shouted Andy as Alice looked him in the eyes when she gave her answer.

"NEVER!" shouted Alice.

"Then I'm sorry it came to this!" said Andy as he started pulling down really hard, and Alice struggled to keep her grip on the cliff.

"ANDY!" suddenly shouted a voice from above.

Alice and Andy both looked up. It was Billy standing at the top of the cliff holding Andy's gun.

"Let her go, Andy!" said Billy.

"Or what? Are you going to shoot me?!" said Andy.

"If I have to. Let. her. go!" said Billy as Andy surprisingly obeyed and let go of Alice's ankle.

"Come on, Billy, we were on the same side about the gold; it's caused us nothing but trouble. Just let me have it, and all our problems will be over," said Andy.

Billy didn't respond.

"You won't kill me, Billy. We're brothers after all (BANG)" Billy fired the gun, hitting Andy in the shoulder and watching him fall into the sea.

"You're not my brother anymore," said Billy. Alice breathed a big sigh of relief, which then turned to panic again, and her left hand lost its grip on the cliff.

"Billy, help!" shouted Alice.

"Alice, give me your hand, come on, reach up!" shouted Billy as both of them stretched their arms out.

Just as Alice's right hand lost its grip, Billy grabbed her.

"I've got you, now your other hand!" said Billy as Alice reached out, and Billy grabbed hold.

Now, with both hands, he pulled her up to safety.

They both fell to the ground and breathed heavily from what had just happened.

"Billy, you saved my life," said Alice.

"Yeah, I guess that makes us even" said Billy.

Alice looked over the cliff to the waves below.

"Do you think he's still alive?" asked Alice.

"Well, he's cheated death once; I don't see why he can't do it again. Mind you, he can't swim very well," said Billy.

"Hey, how did you know I was in trouble?" asked Alice.

"I started to regain consciousness just before you ran away; I saw you knock down Andy, very impressive. When he left and didn't pick up his gun, I took it and gave chase along the top of the cliffs," said Billy.

"But, the pathway was flooded; how did you get past?" asked Alice.

"Easy, I CAN swim," said Billy as he and Alice lay there for a moment before bursting into laughter.

Some sort of hilarity from what Billy said and also great relief that it was finally over.

Millstone on Sea Police Station, Morning, 8:00 am.

Alice, Lucy and Billy were brought to the police station again to discuss what happened during the night. They all explained Andy's desire for revenge, as he blamed the squad for leaving him behind, but they left out the part about the gold, and thankfully, the police and the army bought what they told them. To everyone's surprise, Andy was fished out of the water by one of the Home Guard coastal patrols and arrested; he was taken to the hospital and kept under guard until MI6 came and picked him up. It appeared that Andy had been under their radar after they monitored his return to British soil.

Alice, Lucy and Billy were with the Chief Inspector in his office.

"It appears that Millstone is once again thankful to the three of you. Not only did you find a dreaded spy in our midst, but you also uncovered one of Hitler's collaborators, both of which caused this town great distress," said the Chief.

"Thank you, Chief, we're just glad that it's all over," said Alice.

"As are we," said the Chief.

"If I can just ask, what's going to happen to Andy?" asked Billy.

"Well, there will definitely be a trial after MI6 finishes interrogating him, possibly followed by a firing squad. However, I heard that the Medical Corp is fighting for Andy to be treated instead of shot, so we'll have to see," said the Chief, who got up from his desk.

"Now, girls, I spoke to the Mayor and the town council, and they asked me to reward both of your efforts in Millstone by giving you these," said the Chief as he reached into his desk and pulled out two silver police badges and handed them to the girls.

"Are these really for us?" asked Lucy.

"They are. Unofficially, you're both too young for employment, and there still aren't that many female recruits yet. But I think that they'll help people know who the Millstone Investigators are," said the Chief.

"Thank you, Chief, we really love these," said Alice.

"Billy, didn't the army give you a reward for helping us?" asked Lucy.

"Oh yeah, they did. A gift voucher for Woolworths," said Billy as everyone laughed.

"Okay, guys, I think it's best we let the Chief get back to work," said Alice. She, Lucy, and Billy all got up, said their byes to the Chief, and left the office.

They reconvened at the front of the police station.

"You know, Alice, when this case first started, all we were doing was looking for whoever attacked Tyler. I never thought for a minute that we'd uncover a Nazi spy and a collaborator," said Lucy.

"Well, as it says in the books, Sherlock and Watson never really have a simple case. There's always something else around the corner," said Alice.

"Thank you, Lucy. I don't think I ever said it enough. I'm really glad to have you as my best friend and John Watson," said Alice.

"It's always a pleasure to work with you, Sherlock," said Lucy as they both hugged each other.

"And thank you too, Billy. We might not have got this result without you," said Alice.

"Well, Tyler is my brother, always have been. And I promised him to look after you; I keep my promises," said Billy as Alice and Lucy hugged him.

"So, what's going to happen to you? Are you going back to the front?" asked Alice.

"I don't know yet. Need to wait for my medical test to come back on my head wound. If it's possible that I have a concussion, it'll give me grounds for a medical discharge," said Billy.

"It's the same for Tyler as well. They say once he's recovered, it's likely he won't be able to go back with his injuries," said Alice.

"Well, I always fancied myself in a Home Guard uniform," said Billy.

"Come on, girls, Jasper should have breakfast ready by now," said Billy as they all started walking away.

"So, school is still closed; what are we doing for the rest of the day?" asked Lucy.

"I say we just take it in our stride, Lucy. We may get another case or have earned the day off. It's only elementary," said Alice, and everyone laughed.

The Sergeant watched them from the station entrance with the Chief.

"I don't think that's the last we've seen of them, sir," said the Sergeant.

"I think you're right, Sergeant. But one thing's certain, Millstone is in safe hands, so long as those hands are Alice Sherlock and Lucy Porter," said the Chief.

Chapter 19

Wedded Bliss

<u>1 Year Later</u>

It's 1942, and the war is still raging. There is no sign of Germany giving up, but no sign of Britain doing it either. The town of Millstone had been calmed, and the people were carrying on with their lives as normally as they could. Air raids have become less frequent with the removal of Tim, and Tyler and Billy were given their medical discharges and allowed to join the Home Guard, which they both loved.

Andy was put on trial for his crimes, but the Medical Corps won their right to treat him. Instead of having him executed, he was taken to a mental institution. However, only after a month, Andy was found in his room, and he'd succumbed to his injuries. But the research they did into his burns is believed to hopefully go a long way to developing medicine to help other burn victims. Andy's death wasn't in vain.

Millstone had one other reason to be happy today. As the sound of church bells rang out and a lot of people were gathered inside, it was a truly happy day.

Tyler and Veronica's wedding.

"Wilt thou have this woman to thy wedded wife, to live together after God's

Ordinance in the holy estate of matrimony? Wilt thou love her, comfort her,

Honour and keep her in sickness and in health, and forsaking all others, keep

thee only unto her, so long as ye both shall live?" spoke the Vicar

"I will," said Tyler, looking miles better; with the addition of a walking stick for the occasional weakness in the legs, he was fine the rest of the time.

"Wilt thou have this man to thy wedded husband, to live together after God's

Ordinance, in the holy estate of matrimony? Wilt thou obey him and serve him,

Love, honour, and keep him, in sickness and in health, and forsaking all other

Keep thee only unto him, so long as ye both shall live?" spoke the Vicar.

"Oh, you bet I will," said Veronica, looking fabulous in her wedding dress, which her mother previously wore.

"Then by the power vested in me, in the name of the Father, the Son, and the Holy Ghost, I now pronounce you man and wife. You may kiss the bride," said the vicar as Tyler and Veronica kissed, and the church erupted into applause.

Alice and Lucy were both bridesmaids, and Billy was the best man. Most of their friends had come to the wedding; even Trevor and Coltan were there. Trevor had since made amends with Michelle after she had herself smuggled out of France to be with him. And Coltan was recovering well from his addiction, thanks to the treatments of the mental hospital, not as bad as he thought.

Everyone left the church and went to the reception in the church hall. It was not too big of a splash with there being a war on, but it was still something to marvel at. Tyler and Veronica were going around, hugging and shaking hands with everyone. Old Boy was there, Mr Prosser, Doctor Arthur, Mavis and Jack, and many others. Alice and Lucy were enjoying some of the sweets that Tyler made sure were available, including ration chocolate, Alice's favourite.

"Be careful with that chocolate; you'll get a stomach ache?" said Billy.

"Sorry," said Alice.

"Ah, what better day for there to be than that of a wedding?" said Trevor as he came over, arm in arm with Michelle, a very pretty girl in her early thirties.

"Weddings are so rushed in France, everyone thinks they need to be hitched in case they die tomorrow. It's nice to see one that's all about true love," said Michelle with a strong French accent.

"Who knows, maybe that'll be us one day," said Trevor.

"Who knows indeed, mon amie. Now then, maybe you could show me where the crypt is; I'd really like to know how dark and empty it is," said Michelle as she pulled Trevor away.

"Oh la, la," said Trevor as he left.

"It's funny, isn't it? He gets the French girl, and what do I get? Several months in a mental hospital, it doesn't seem fair," said Coltan as he came over.

"Well, if it helps you feel more normal again, maybe you can see that as getting a better deal," said Billy.

"Yeah, I suppose so," said Coltan as someone else came over, someone they weren't expecting.

"Hey, Coltan, that wine they've got is fantastic. It's made of grapes, can you believe it?" said a very drunk Wesley.

"Who invited you?" asked Lucy.

"I did. Well, Tyler said we can invite friends," said Coltan.

"You're friends with him?!" asked Billy.

"Yeah, turns out he's not such an arsehole once you get to know him", said Coltan.

"Yeah. Wait, what?" said Wesley.

"Come on, mate, I'll get you another glass of that wine," said Coltan as he walked Wesley away.

Alice was about to say something.

"Don't say anything. Just...eat your chocolate," said Billy.

"You okay, Alice?" asked Lucy.

"Yeah, I'm really good. It's days like this that remind you not everything is doom and gloom," said Alice.

"Yeah, you're right. Tyler looks happy and healthy; he and Veronica make a good match," said Lucy.

"Yeah, they're going to be okay," said Billy.

Alice put her plate down on the table.

"I'm just going to step outside for a moment; I think that chocolate is getting to me a bit," said Alice as she walked away.

"He told you to be careful," said Lucy.

Alice stepped out into this garden area outside the church hall, with a few flower beds and some benches. It was supposed to be for peace and tranquillity; at least, that's what the vicar always said. Alice sat down for a moment until she suddenly heard a familiar voice.

"We meet again, Alice," said Sherlock Holmes.

"Mr Holmes, I haven't seen you for a while. I thought that you'd left after the case concluded," said Alice.

"I just thought it was time to step away for a while. Allow yourself to bask in the victory and keep using all the new skills you learned for good. And I have to say, I'm very impressed," said Sherlock.

"You did really well, Alice. You checked every angle, every clue, you double-checked and triple-checked, you looked for the gaps in the stories, and most of all, you didn't give up," said Sherlock.

"Intelligence, brawn, brute force and the occasional use of a revolver. All valuable traits in an investigator and your friends performed their roles with courage, like my dear friend Watson," said Sherlock.

"But it wasn't just my friends or the skills. You had a hand in it, too, Mr Holmes, always giving me advice at the right time and stopping me from giving up. I'm grateful," said Alice.

"Now you do sound like Watson. Always telling me what a great detective I am and a good friend," said Sherlock.

"Speaking of which, I'm sorry to tell you this, Alice, I shall be returning to London for a while. But I believe that you've learned a lot, and there's still more to come. Millstone is in good hands," said Sherlock.

"I understand, Mr Holmes, and thank you for everything," said Alice.

"Miss Sherlock," said Sherlock.

"Mr Holmes," said Alice as Sherlock started to walk away.

"Wait, Mr Holmes. Will I ever see you again?" asked Alice.

"Of course, you will; you know where to find me," said Sherlock as he pointed to his head, then walked away and disappeared in front of Alice.

She felt a slight tear running down her cheek.

"Alice," said Lucy.

Alice quickly wiped the tears as Lucy and Billy both came over.

"Just came to see if you were okay," said Lucy.

"Yeah, I'm good. Feeling a little better now," said Alice.

"Well, we should think of heading back inside. The dancing is about to start, and that blonde-haired bridesmaid has her eye on me," said Billy.

"You know, something still bothers me. Even though we found Tim and Andy, to this day, we still don't know what happened to all that gold," said Lucy.

"Yeah, you're right. (Alice reached into a pocket on her dress and pulled out the letter with the riddle). I still carry this letter with me; every day when I'm alone, I look at it and try to figure out what it means, but I still haven't," said Alice.

"Let me have a read", said Billy as Alice handed him the letter, and he read it.

"Eagles....Dragon's cave....Guardian, ha, ha," said Billy with a laugh at the end.

"What's funny?" asked Alice.

"Oh, nothing. It's just when I first found my cave; I used to think it was so big that a dragon must've lived there at one point," said Billy as Alice and Lucy looked at each other with surprise.

"And I suppose I think of myself as the guardian; it is my place, after all, I....." Billy stopped when he looked at Alice and Lucy.

"What, what is it?" asked Billy as they both turned to look at him.

"Billy, think about what you just said, then read the letter again," said Alice.

"I said that when I first found my cave, I thought that a....dragon...and I'm the....guardian", said Billy as it started to dawn on him.

"No bloody way," said Billy.

"It makes sense; the one place to hide the gold was right under everyone's noses," said Alice.

"The smuggler must've moved it there before Tyler and Billy left the front. That's what the letter was all about; he was telling Tyler where to find it," said Lucy.

"So what do we do, tell Tyler and get some shovels?" asked Billy as the music started inside the hall.

"Maybe we'll tell him afterwards. Come on, everyone, let's dance," said Alice as she and Lucy ran back inside.

"Wait for me," said Billy as he ran to catch up.

The case was solved, and Millstone was safe once again. Tyler recovered, and the rest of the squad learned a lot from their experiences. Life returned to normal in the coastal town.

But as for the case of the missing gold, all they had to do was look right under their noses.

And dig deep.

The End

Printed in Great Britain
by Amazon